Richard E. Drdek grew up in the Cleveland he describes in THE GAME and attended college at Cleveland State University. He joined the Air Corps after Pearl Harbor as a navigator. After his plane crashed in the jungles of northern Brazil, his crew, escaping serious injury, was rescued by a Navy blimp. He returned to civilian life and received a Master of Science in Education. He has taught in the classroom and has writtten beginning reading books. At present he is Assistant Professor of Elementary Education at a New York State College. THE GAME is his first book for children in the middle grades.

THE GAME

THE GAME

Richard E. Drdek

Doubleday & Company, Inc.
Garden City, New York

Library of Congress Catalog Card Number 68–14182

To the memory of Bob

THE GAME

1

The boy looked at the shoe box filled with five- and ten-dollar bills, and then he looked through the elderberry bushes toward the figure of his uncle sitting on the rocks, fishing. His first impulse was to run to the rocks and triumphantly announce his good fortune. He fought the urge. To run and tell his uncle would be too easy. It would be too easy on his uncle. The game! He'd have to play the game. If the situation were turned around—if it were the uncle who had a surprise, there'd be a game. Every birthday present, every Christmas present, or any special gift was always introduced by a game. There always was much teasing and the slow build-up of suspense. The uncle always built the boy's curiosity to the breaking point. For once, he, the boy, could be the boss of the game. He could establish the dialogue and set the rules. But how?

He let his gaze circle the area as if to find a clue. In front of him was the calm and blue Lake Erie. Far in the distance on the other side of the breakwater was the shape of a ship trailing a black cloud of smoke on its way to some place named and located on a map. A tug was towing a barge toward the lighthouse which marked the entrance to the harbor. To his right he could see the skyline of downtown Cleveland dominated by the Terminal Tower's silver dome shimmering in the glare of a midmorning in August. Almost behind him was the High Level Bridge. Rising almost one hundred feet above the river's valley, its network of steel in its high-tension arch was but a pattern of thin lines drawn on a light blue sky. The boy could see the shapes, mere shadows, of streetcars gliding through the lower level while on top, cars and trucks sped to and from the downtown section.

Sonny Novak had never been on that bridge. He had never ridden one of the streetcars which flowed through the bottom level. Often he had wondered where the cars and trucks were going. As he watched them, and he frequently did, he felt a kind of urgency in their speed, and he fashioned for them an idea of unfettered freedom. To Sonny, a car was no mere vehicle; it was a passport to roads and highways that led to unexplored forests, to un-climbed mountains, and to uncharted rivers. A car was not a piece of machinery; it was an exit to the city and an entrance to a world of nature beyond. A car was all these things, but not for himself. A car meant an exit and a passport for his uncle, a chance to be Marco Polo. For his uncle a car could be the ticket to hundreds of tiny lakes and streams beyond the sidewalks and streetcar tracks of Cleveland.

The car, the boy decided, would be the game. The money in the shoe box would buy the car that would enable the uncle to break loose from his small world which was limited by what he could walk in a day or how far he could go on the Cleveland Railway Company's streetcars and buses. Yes, the boy concluded, a car would please his uncle most. His uncle needed a car.

Stuffing the shoe box into his knapsack, Sonny walked casually out of the bushes, across the sand, and onto the short finger of rocks which stretched from the beach into the lake. As he approached the spot where his uncle sat, he was mindful of the mushrooms, the mushrooms he and his uncle had picked early that morning in the grassy area of the beach and which the uncle had arranged precisely on the rocks for drying.

"How you doing?" the boy asked with studied nonchalance, taking up his own fishing pole.

"Got three bullheads. One is a good sizer. Two are puny ones."

"How about my line?"

"Yes, how about it?"

"What did my line catch?"

"Your line was perfectly safe. Fish won't bite on a dead line."

"It's your dumplings," said the boy. "I don't blame the fish. I only eat them so's not to hurt your feelings. The fish just aren't as polite. Or maybe they're more honest."

"Dumplings are good bait," the uncle maintained, keeping up the make-believe argument. "See, I have caught three. But bait alone never catches fish. It's the man who dangles the hook. Only a dreamer throws out bait and leaves the work to the gods."

"You have two hands. Why didn't you jiggle my hook?"

"I had no idea that my nephew was such a lazy Jack. And I see that you brought no elderberries back."

"They weren't ready yet," the boy replied. "The Little People hadn't expected us so soon."

"When do you think that the Little People will ripen them for us?"

"Maybe in another week."

"Will they provide us with enough for a half-dozen jars of jelly?"

"At least enough for two pies."

"Mmmm," the uncle considered. "But a half-dozen jars of jelly in the pantry will mean a sweeter breakfast during the long winter months. You would wipe out a pie in one day."

The boy slapped his flat stomach. "I'll take the pie in one sitting. You can have the jelly all during the winter."

The old man sighed remorsefully for the boy's benefit. "That's why the old must take care of the young. The old can think in terms of seasons and years; the young cannot get beyond the day."

"It's unfair," complained the boy, humorously.

"What is?"

"The old always throw in wise sayings in order to win an argument or for an excuse for something they're going to do."

"That's because the old were dreamers who discovered that dreams are for fairy tales. They know that the fish in the skillet are the only ones that matter and not the fish in the lake."

The boy seized upon that line as a chance to start his game.

"What if," the boy said, measuring his words, "all the fish in the lake were yours, what then?"

"I'd die for a bowl of beef stew."

Two men in a rowboat drew up within shouting distance of the rocks.

"Getting anything?" the man at the oars called.

"Bullheads," the uncle replied, holding up his string of three.

"Ugh," said the man. "What happened to all the pike and perch we used to catch?"

The men in the boat rowed toward the uncle on the rocks. Fishermen, Sonny decided, seem to belong to a kind of club. Whenever two men with fishing tackle meet, it's as if they've known each other all their lives. Two fishermen are never strangers. Get three of them together, and they hold a meeting.

Sonny made a mental note of his observation so that he

could tease his uncle about it sometime. But now he was sorry that the men had interrupted his game. It meant that he would have to start it all over again.

"It might be the weather," the uncle replied to the question. "We've had weeks of hot, muggy weather. The water's hot. All of the good eating fish have gone out where the lake is deep, and they're hanging around on the bottom where the water's still cool."

"You know what I think?" the man trolling in the back of the boat suggested. "I think that it's this crazy depression. The fish only bite two days a week—the two days I work."

"I wish we had a motor for this tub," said the man at the oars. "I'd get on the other side of the breakwater and do some deep trolling. I'd go into their cool hide-out and dangle the bait in front of their noses."

"What we need is a good storm," said the uncle. "A good hard blow from the northwest would churn this pond up a bit and mix some of the hot surface water with the cooler water underneath."

Sonny waited patiently for the men to solve the fishing problem and get on their way. The money was agitating him. He wanted very much to present his find to his uncle. The men in the boat were making it difficult for him. He might not be able to restrain himself for the sake of the game. He thought for a while that the men in the boat would exchange greetings with his uncle and then go. But now they were talking about their jobs. Both men apparently worked together in a foundry.

"Instead of laying off a whole gang," the oarsman was saying, "the boss divides up the work so we each get in about two days a week. We ain't starving, but a guy with a family can't make much headway on two days' pay."

Unable to stand the strain any longer and having no

interest in the conversation, Sonny got to his feet and walked the rocks back to the beach. The white sand glistened in the sun. The surface of the lake was calm and smooth, looking as if it had been painted there on some huge canvas. The only movement was a motorboat, cruising slowly along the far side of the breakwater. Sonny wondered how much a boat with a motor would cost. Maybe his uncle would like to have one so he could fish in the deep part of the lake. Would he have enough money for both a car and a boat? Of course, the car was the most important item. A boat was just for fishing; a car was for everything.

Sonny walked along, kicking the sand. One time he had found a fountain pen on the beach. He had kicked it up. The pen was a big fat red one with a gold point. He had offered it to his uncle, believing that a pen in his shirt pocket would make his uncle look important, but his uncle had refused to accept it. Sonny had put it into his cigar box of treasures. He meant to get some ink one day and see how well the pen wrote. That the pen might not be any good never entered Sonny's mind. The fact that the pen had a fourteen-karat gold point was enough to prevent the raising of any doubts. Gold meant the finest, and the finest was the finest, wasn't it?

As he walked through the sand, kicking up surf-flattened stones, clamshells, empty cigarette packs, and the other debris humans like to discard on beaches, he saw something shiny. At first he thought that it was a silver dollar. He dived at it and discovered that he had uncovered a toy. On one side was a mirror. The other side held a glassed-in game. Under the glass was a clown's face with two pits for eyes. Free to roll about were two BB shots. Sonny guessed that the idea was to get the two BB's into the eye sockets. He accomplished this almost immediately.

He then turned it over and looked at himself in the little mirror. The reflection was distorted because of the cheapness of the glass, so he made faces at himself while rotating the mirror to see the results. Several times he chuckled at what he saw.

Tiring of that, he turned back toward the rocks and caught the morning sunlight in the glass. The mirror threw a disc of brightness into the shadows of the rocks. Off in the distance was the lighthouse that marked the entrance to the Cuyahoga River. He shot a reflection of the sun at the glass windows at the top of the lighthouse. Satisfied that he could signal for help in case of distress, he put the toy into his pocket. He would take it with him everywhere he went. Mentally he ran over several emergencies which might develop and which would call for the services of a signaling device. For instance, a storm suddenly comes up and the two men in the boat are tossed under by huge waves. Out comes the mirror. He flashes a distress message to the lighthouse keeper. Help comes in the nick of time.

"No," he said to himself, erasing the story. "If there was a storm, there'd be no sun."

His mind next painted a picture of a girl swimmer far out from shore, calling for help. A signal? No! He would jump in and save her. He could see himself carrying her limp form out of the water and onto the beach. Is she still alive? Is she still breathing? The mirror! He puts the mirror against her mouth. Her faint breath clouds the glass. She lives!

A glance in the direction of the rocks told him that the men in the boat were leaving. He started back toward his uncle. What a wonderful morning it had been! A boxful of money and a lifesaving toy! He wondered just how much money there was. He decided that there must be at least a thousand dollars in the box. Now he must get on with the game.

As he took his place next to his uncle, he said, "The Little People were good to me. Guess what the Little People gave me."

"A diamond tiara for you to give to an Arabian princess whom you will no doubt marry."

"No, but you're close."

"A Yo-yo!"

"You're getting warmer."

"A genuine imitation of a reproduction of the Mona Lisa."

"You're so close that you've almost got it."

"I give up."

With great delight, the boy put the toy into the palm of his hand with the clown's face upward and held it out to his uncle.

Without picking it up, the uncle said, "Turn it over and you'll see a fool or a philosopher."

Quickly, without thinking, Sonny flipped it over and when he saw his own reflection, he laughed at having been tricked so easily. The uncle pulled the boy's hand over to him and looked at the mirror.

"I saw a philosopher," he chuckled. "Which did you see?"

"I see a wisecracking uncle; that's what I see."

Sonny felt that although he had not done too well at that game he would take charge with the money. While he considered how best to get into the game, his uncle spoke.

"You know what I've been thinking?" the uncle said with a sigh. "I've got to find some kind of a job."

"A job? Why?"

"We simply won't make it through the winter unless I can get some kind of steady income. You've grown out of

your clothes, and soon school will be starting. Our coal
shed is empty. The flour bin has about a cupful in it.
We'll either freeze to death or starve to death. Which
would you prefer?"

"I'll take freezing. I'd hate to die hungry."

"Good! We'll be the fattest frozen corpses in the
morgue."

The boy asked apprehensively, "Your shop isn't doing
too well?"

"I haven't had a paying customer in weeks."

The boy swallowed hard. "What will you do?"

"I'll see if I can't get some kind of WPA job. With luck
I might be able to land something that will pay twelve or
fifteen dollars a week."

"But that'll mean you'll be gone all day every day,"
Sonny complained.

"It's got to be done," the uncle said firmly. "You're a
big boy now. You can take care of yourself."

"But think of all the fun we have together," Sonny
pleaded, unable to keep the hurt and the bitterness from
his voice. "With you working all day every day, we can't
go fishing or mushrooming or just scrounging around."

"It'll just have to be, that's all. You don't need me any
more to keep you out of mischief. You need good grub
and clothes and books. And it's about time that I shoved
you out of the nest and got you going on your own."

"It's not me so much, Unk," the boy rationalized. "It's
you I'm thinking about. You'd die on a job like that. You
won't be happy tied down to a job."

"I lived like that for years before I inherited you," the
uncle reminded him with a grin.

"Don't do anything yet," said the boy now seeing the
money as playing a different role. "Something might come
up. You may be surprised."

"I know," said the uncle. "Lawyer Maresh will come knocking on my door and say, 'Mr. Novak, sir, your very rich cousin, Matilda, has gone to the great bye-bye and has left all her yachts and gold mines to you because she was sorry that she never got to know you.'"

The boy laughed, happy to see his uncle shift from the very serious mood he was in. It also meant that he could get back to the game.

"Who's Cousin Matilda?" he demanded, egging his uncle on.

"Waltzing Matilda, she was called. About fifty years ago she waltzed westward toward the Rockies and waltzed herself into the biggest gold mine in the world."

"What about her husband? Isn't there a Mr. Waltzing Matilda?"

"No. Funny thing about the old gal. She just could never stop gyrating long enough for a preacher to tie the knot."

"So now you're rich," said Sonny. "What will you do with the money?"

The uncle shook his head despairingly. Sonny was afraid that his uncle would leave the game and get serious again.

"What if you really had all the money you wanted?"

"Impossible," the uncle snorted. "No man has all the money he wants. He finds ten dollars, and he regrets that he didn't find twenty. He accumulates ten million, and he's sorry he couldn't have piled up twenty million. Give a beggar a dime and he'll tell you what he could do if he had a quarter."

The boy was exasperated. The game wasn't going as he had planned, so he tried a new attack.

"Let's say you had a thousand dollars. What then?"

"I'd open a bank."

"No! How would you spend a thousand dollars?"

"I would buy a suit of armor and marry a princess. I would live in a castle and make you my court jester."

"Ask me what I would do," the boy demanded. "Go ahead and ask me."

"What would a mentally retarded urchin like you do with a thousand dollars?"

"I would buy for you a Ford car like the monsignor has."

"What would an old fool like me do with a Ford car? If God had meant me to ride, He would have given me wheels instead of feet."

"You could get into your Ford car and drive out to the country. You could fish in one of those lakes like Pasek the butcher goes to. Maybe you could catch something besides bullheads and carp. You could go out into the woods to look for your mushrooms."

The uncle was somewhat taken aback by the boy's unselfish concern for him.

"A car is a pest," the old man pretended to grumble. "It runs you. The driver gets to see only the concrete in front of him. When I go, I like to feel the sunshine on my back and hear the birds sing."

"We could get you one with a top that folds down."

"So I have a Ford car? It's a monster. It guzzles gasoline and oil. I once knew a man who thought he had a tiger for a pet. He had to feed all his sheep to the tiger. Some people, fools no doubt, said that the tiger had the man for a slave."

The boy was rescued from the turn the discussion had taken by a frantic bobbing of the cork on his line. He played it like an expert while his uncle watched anxiously. Finally the boy pulled in his prize.

"A carp!" he said with disgust. "Wouldn't you know." He unhooked it and flung it back into the lake. Baiting his hook again, he added, "Is there anything here worth catching?"

The uncle measured the height of the sun, and being satisfied with its angle, opened his knapsack. He took out a loaf of the rye bread he had baked the day before and a small piece of smoked summer sausage. With his knife (he had made it from a fine piece of tool steel and had cast on it an aluminum handle) he carved two thick slices from the loaf.

As Sonny eagerly tore into the bread, he said, "I would buy you a fine watch like the one you used to have."

The old man was surprised that the boy had remembered the gold watch. It was almost five years ago that he had sold it to Kortanek the interurban streetcar conductor. Kortanek had dropped his own, and a conductor's job depended upon an accurate watch.

"If you had a watch you'd know when to feed me," the boy went on. "How much did Kortanek give you for your watch?"

"Six dollars."

"It was worth much more."

"Not really. He needed the watch, and I needed six dollars. It was a fair trade."

"When the watch disappeared, I got a sheepskin coat," the boy reflected. "So if I had the money, I would buy you another watch just like it."

"A watch is for a man with appointments or a schedule to meet," the uncle snorted, and cut the sausage in half.

Accepting his share, the boy continued, "I'd pack you off to Dr. Mikesh and get you fitted with a pair of spectacles. Every time you use that butcher knife of yours, I expect you to carve your thumb off."

The uncle laughed as he replaced the knife in its scabbard.

"What spectacles I could get for a thousand dollars! On a gold stick studded with diamonds maybe."

Uncorking his canteen, he sipped some of the tepid tea and passed the flask to the boy.

"A fishing rod with a reel," Sonny continued, enjoying the game now. "Maybe a boat. Would you like a boat so you could go out into the lake and drag a line in the deep, cool water to get where the big perch hang out?"

"No, I would not like a boat or a rod and reel. If you must buy me something, buy me a job so I can make a decent living for us."

Now Sonny was sure that the game was going his way. Very seriously he said, "Then I would give you the thousand dollars and you wouldn't need a job. You could have the Ford car to run around in, wearing your new spectacles, and forget about a job for maybe another year. You could buy the coal and flour you need and not worry about what you make in the shop."

With an expression of great sadness, the man said to his ward, "If wishes were Fords, every beggar would ride. We can't buy coal and flour with wishes. We need the real stuff. We need legitimate U.S. currency. The sooner you accept that the better. So let's end this foolish game."

Slowly and deliberately, Sonny withdrew the shoe box from his knapsack. With a flourish, he swung the cover off and presented the money to his uncle's view.

"Look what else the Little People left for me," he said.

2

About three miles away, to the south and east of where the two were fishing, a street named Broadway begins. In 1935, long before superhighways and cloverleaf interchanges became a part of the city's landscape, Broadway began near the Cuyahoga River, wandered through the industrial flats, snaked out of the valley, and carved a meandering path southeasterly through the city. It was the road which anyone who wanted to go to Pittsburgh took to Pittsburgh. Where Broadway emerged from the valley stood a church, its stones made grimy by years and years of smoke and soot from the valley's industrial furnaces. For almost a hundred years, the church had been the center of a city within a city. More than a thousand houses clustered around the church, simple houses, small, one-story frame dwellings without basements. Behind each house was a coal shed for the fuel that fed the stoves which heated the houses. Not every house in 1935 boasted the luxury of an inside bathroom.

The people who settled in that area, built their homes there, built their church, and created the city within a city, had begun migrating from Bohemia in the 1840s. Some were from the cities, such as Prague and Pilsen. Most were of peasant stock. All had come to Cleveland, seeking the rewards of the city's industries. They brought with them their customs, their songs, and their traditions. As more and more Bohemian immigrants arrived they settled among those who knew their ways and spoke the same language. So the city within the city grew. In 1935, first-, second-, third-, and fourth-generation Czechs were living there.

The church was the center, the hub of the community, and one of the most influential persons was the parish priest. People moved into the neighborhood, and some moved out. Children were born there. There were deaths. Houses burned down from overheated stoves and were rebuilt. The population changed, but not the church. True, a tornado had struck the community, knocking down the church's famous bell towers, but the church never really changed. Part of the reason for its stability was the constant influx of new immigrants who saw in the church a touch of their old world. The priest then became their counselor and trusted friend as well as spiritual leader.

While the boy and his uncle were eating their mid-morning snack, the pastor of the church, having completed a nine o'clock requiem high mass, was out walking his dog. He was walking up Broadway, enjoying his first cigar of the day. Mopsy, enjoying her freedom, pranced ahead of him, sniffing a route she knew very well. The dog knew that they were on their way to Pasek's meat market, and something told her that a special treat was to be had there.

Mopsy got to the door of the store first and waited patiently for her master to open the door. Once inside, the dog walked slowly to the far end of the counter and sat down at attention. The priest was about to answer the butcher's greeting when he noticed someone else in the shop. It was the neighborhood's chief busybody, the greatest living authority on right and wrong, the parish's conscience by her own appointment. She was called "Baba Chlepna," Grandmother Gossip. The priest sensed that she had been waiting there for him and that he had walked into her trap. He regretted having established the habit of stopping at the butcher shop while on his morning walks.

"Monsignor," she began, "I must talk to you."

"Confessions are heard on Saturdays," he said lightly, winking at the butcher.

"This is a parish matter, Monsignor," she replied.

"Then why not see me in the parish home?"

"I never seem to find you in."

The priest blushed slightly. He had been aware that she was wanting to see him, but he didn't think that his dodging her had been so obvious.

"Why not make an appointment?" he suggested kindly.

She laughed, a rich musical chuckle. "What I have to say is not in the least bit personal. It's the talk of the whole parish. It's about that Novak boy."

The butcher noticed that at the mention of the name the priest grew taut.

"Oh," said the monsignor. "Indeed?"

"That boy just can't go on living with that man. We've got to do something. I'm sure that with your help we can go to the juvenile court and get that boy away from that shiftless man."

"What's the matter with where that boy's living?" the priest demanded almost belligerently.

"The boy is twelve now. He's growing into a young man."

"So?"

"They live together in that shop, in one little room."

"I've seen it. What's wrong with the place?"

"A growing boy needs more room. He needs a place where he can study and a place where he can bring his friends."

"Come now, Mrs. Hronek," the priest laughed. "You're

being a bit dramatic. I grew up in a five-room shack with twelve kids in the family. I had friends, and I studied."

"It's more than that, Monsignor. Have you watched them together? They're like two children. You can't tell which one is raising whom."

Leonard started to wrap the bones but leaned on the chopping block instead. He started to say something but clamped his mouth shut. He expected the priest to reply. But the old lady plunged on.

"And those wild stories the old man has that boy believing! Imaginary people that spread out mushrooms and berries for them to pick up! I've heard them."

"What's wrong with stories? God gave man an imagination so that he could create and glorify Him."

"Imagination is fine, but we live in a world of reality—a world of laws."

"I'm afraid that I don't understand," said the priest. The old lady shook her head as if she couldn't believe her ears.

"That poor boy doesn't have a decent pair of trousers to cover his legs. His toes stick out of his shoes. And how does the boy eat? Neither of the two knows where their next meal is coming from. And what about the boy's character? Like two children they are at play together. How can he instruct the boy in responsibility when he acts like a child himself?"

The priest and the butcher, both, had long been aware of the close ties between Frank and the boy, but neither had thought much of it. The butcher turned to the priest, hoping to hear from him a reply which would satisfy the woman and reassure him.

"What are you suggesting?" the priest said, and Leonard felt that the woman had scored her mark.

"That you lead your group of responsible parishioners

and put our case before the judge of the juvenile court. We must protect that boy. It's the monsignor's holy duty."

"Then what do we do with the boy? Give him to you to raise?"

"Parmadale," she said.

"No."

"Last Sunday in the monsignor's beautiful sermon you told us of the wonderful work being done at the orphanage. The boy belongs there."

"No," said the priest in almost a whisper.

"But, Monsignor, we must think of the boy. We must think what is best for him."

"No. I will not be a part of any such stupid scheme."

"The monsignor is forcing us to take the matter in our own hands. We will see the judge ourselves."

"You would be doing a great wrong."

"The monsignor ought to hear what the ladies in our group have witnessed. They will tell you of the neglect, how Frank lets that boy grow like a weed. Like two children living together they are, playing games. How can that man bring up that boy when he can't even set an example? How can that boy have any respect for him?"

"The boy stays with his uncle."

"We are collecting statements from many responsible people who are concerned over the boy's welfare. If the monsignor will just read those statements, he will see."

"All right. You bring me the testimony, and I shall examine it. Heaven help anyone who bears false witness against his neighbor."

"Thank you, Monsignor," she said almost triumphantly. "That's all we want: to be given a fair hearing. Good day, Monsignor."

"May God go with you, Mrs. Hronek," he responded. She left like a battleship that had taken all the enemy's fire power and had survived it with only her paint scratched. She was withdrawing only to reload.

"A lot she knows," said the butcher, wrapping the bones and tying them with many loops of string so that the dog could carry the package easily. "A boy needs a lot more than pants to cover his backside."

"Why does she have to agitate things?" the priest wondered. "Frank may be too easygoing with the boy, but they're tied together with stronger ties than in most families."

"She's got a new mission in life," the butcher answered. "And you can see Frank two ways. You can think of him as being a kind, overindulgent parent, or you can see him as being too lazy to care about things."

Leonard placed the package of bones in Mopsy's mouth. She stood on her hind legs, pawed the air as her thank you, and trotted to the door.

"Can she do as she says?" asked the butcher. "Can she have the boy taken away from Frank?"

"She can force me to take a stand," replied the priest with a shrug. "She can ask the courts to look into the matter. Let's just say that I'd rather not see this thing made into an issue. If the court or anyone else starts nosing around, somebody's going to be hurt."

The priest laid a dime on the counter to pay for the bones and opened the door for Mopsy.

"I wish I knew more about that evidence she's collecting. Do you know?"

"I haven't got the faintest notion," said the butcher. "But I'll keep my ears open. I'm for Frank all the way."

"The kid or Frank or both would have had to do something very serious to attract the attention of the courts. They haven't come into a sudden flood of money lately?

Frank isn't tossing money around like he's Diamond Jim
Brady?"

"If he has, he's not been throwing any of it my way,"
the butcher laughed. "But I'll keep a lookout."

"Thanks."

Smiling and waving, the priest went out, but instead of
going home as Mopsy had expected, he turned toward
Fiftieth Street. There, among a number of very old houses
was Frank's shop. It suddenly looked very small to the
priest. Across its single plate-glass window was printed,
"Frank Novak's Fixit Shop." He strode to the door and
opened it. Mopsy bounded in. The old spitz seemed to
know that here, in this building, could be found a boy who
would try to take the package from her. She would have
to play her role as a savage beast and snarl and growl.
Then they would wrestle. Finally the boy would give up,
letting her win.

Eagerly, the dog ran across the floor of the shop and
through the curtains that separated the living quarters
from the shop. After searching every corner of the back
room, Mopsy returned disappointed. Her master was standing in the middle of the shop, trying to relight the cigar
he had so sadly neglected.

"She even ruined my morning smoke," he complained.
"I'm sure that her poor husband has earned his place in
heaven."

Mopsy was wandering about, confused. She had gone to
the front window and was looking out of it as if expecting
her friend to appear at any moment.

"It's Wednesday," the priest said to the dog. "Frank
closes on Wednesday. He and the boy are probably sitting
in God's wonderful sunshine catching God's beautiful fish."

Sitting down on a stool in the shop, the priest glanced
around. The shop was neat, orderly, and clean. Here was a

foot-powered grinding wheel. There was a foot-powered wood-turning lathe. By the window was a motor-driven metal-turning lathe. In a corner was a hand-cranked forge. All were built by Frank Novak by hand out of scraps. The tools—many of them Frank had made himself. Along the walls were cubbyholes in which were filed nuts and bolts and screws and pieces of all kinds of scrap metal.

"Come on, Mopsy. Let's go home."

Outside on the way home, the priest's mind drifted back to another Frank Novak he had known. Both of them had come to the parish twenty-five years ago. He, Father Raymond Jindra, the new young pastor, and Frank Novak, master mechanic at the steel mill, began a new life in the neighborhood. Frank had moved into Mrs. Skala's rooming house, a man of mystery. The ladies thought that he was a sad widower, pining for a lost wife. Some of the widows, of which group Baba Chlepna was one, set out to trap him. But Frank had remained aloof. He worked hard and kept to himself.

Fifteen years had passed. With each year, Frank had become more and more of a mystery. He saw fewer people, was turning more and more into himself. The widows had all but given up on him. In the early 1920s, he had bought a car, a brass-hooded Chevrolet. Every Sunday in the warm months after six o'clock mass, he could be seen heading south on Broadway. Mrs. Skala often complained about having to cook fish, his fish, for him on Sunday nights. Now if he could bring the fish on Friday, it would be all right. But why on Sunday? Mrs. Hronek, Baba Chlepna, wondered with whom he went fishing.

Everyone, even the priest, was surprised when one Sunday in the September of 1925 Frank was not seen at either of the two masses. Mrs. Skala told the neighborhood that Frank had left on the Thursday morning with a packed

suitcase. No one had seen him all that week. The next
Sunday at the ten o'clock mass, Frank was there. But he
was not alone. A small child was with him. Father Jindra
saw him as he mounted the pulpit. There sat Frank with
face drawn and a child's small arms clutched about his
neck. After mass, the priest found the man and the child
waiting for him in the sacristy.

"Can we talk?" Frank asked.

The priest dismissed the altar boys and took the child
from Frank's arms. Indicating a chair for the man, the
priest sat down and rode the child on his knee, to the great
gurgling delight of the child.

"What a happy child!" said the priest. "Where did you
get him?"

"He's my wife's, Father."

The priest turned a surprised look to the man. "Your
wife's? How can it be? You've been a widower for—for how
many years?"

"My wife had left me. Then I moved here. Or that's why
I moved here."

"She left? Was it with somebody else?"

"Yes, Father."

"She divorced you. A civil divorce. And married the
man she went away with?"

"I don't know. He left a wife."

The child had tired of the knee game and had worked
his way into the priest's lap. There he stood with his warm
cheek pressed against the priest's shoulder.

"Poor child," said the priest. "So this must be their
child."

"I don't know, Father."

"What do you mean you don't know? Didn't you ask
her?"

"She was dead. Something she drank."

"I'm all muddled up. I don't understand," the priest said, sighing painfully.

"She had gone with the baby to a rooming house in Chicago. Two days later they found her dead. She had my name and address in her purse." After a moment the man shrugged helplessly. "The police called me."

"No sign of the man?"

"No, Father."

"No idea where she had come from?"

"No, Father."

"Do you suppose the father is the man she went away with?"

The man flapped his arms to convey wonderment. "He left one wife to go off with her."

"The poor child! And the poor mother. She must have suffered too."

The two men looked at each other for a long moment, each expecting the other to say something.

It was the priest who broke the silence. "I'll do whatever I can."

"I'd like you to baptize him, Father."

"He hasn't been baptized? No, you wouldn't know. Yes, I will baptize him."

"Thank you, Father."

"What's his name?"

"I don't know."

Trying to add a cheerful note, the priest chuckled softly, "All right, as the godfather, you pick a name."

"No, I'll have to be the boy's father," the man answered with a positiveness that startled the priest.

The priest shook his head vigorously. "No. No. You can't."

"Yes, I can, Father."

"That's not what I mean. You're capable, yes. You're a

good man, yes. You're sober. You're hard working. You could be a good father to any child. But not this one. No, not this little fellow."

"Why not? Just tell me why not."

"Just because I wear these vestments, it doesn't mean I live in a kind of dreamworld. I know bitterness and hurt. Unless you had married a woman you hated, you were hurt. You were hurt by her leaving."

Painfully, sorry that the conversation had drifted to the topic, the man said, "What has all that got to do with it? All I'm asking is for you to baptize him."

"Now, don't get impatient, Frank. What you're doing— or trying to do—is wonderful, but is it wise?"

"All right, what do you suggest I do with the boy?"

"We have orphanages. Fine ones."

"No!"

"Dedicated people will give him what he needs. . . ."

"No!"

The child had gone to sleep and the priest held him tighter. He fixed his eyes on the man's face and demanded, "Are you trying to punish yourself? Do you blame yourself? Is this child to be your cross? Tell me."

Frank shook his head. "No, Father."

"Then why? Why?"

"He's my wife's. I am her husband. She died and left a child. That's it."

"She left a child of misery, of despair built on broken vows, selfishness, and lust, too. This child is the offspring of your misery, broken dreams, and of days and days and days of loneliness. Tell me, Frank, how could you ever hope to love this poor creature?"

"How, Father, can you think I could hate him? If I am a victim of a wrong, so is he."

The priest sighed again. "I will baptize him. What name would you like?"

"I have always been fond of St. Anthony."

"Ah, yes. The patron of the lost," nodded the priest.

"And the patron of the found, too."

"Wonderful! And what will Anthony's last name be?"

"Novak. The same as mine."

"Oh, Frank. Be reasonable. He's not yours."

"What would you name him, Smith?"

"There must be a birth record some place."

"The police thought so, too. They couldn't trace her."

"They must not have tried. What name did she use in Chicago?"

"Novak. She signed into the rooming house as Mrs. Frank Novak."

"All right, Frank. If that's the way you want it. Let's go to the baptistry."

They walked through the cool, dark, empty church. The sunlight streaming through the stained-glass windows cast colored blocks of light on the stone floors and the pews.

In the baptistry, the priest asked, "What about godparents?"

"Anyone you suggest, Father."

He thought for a moment. "No. I'd have to tell the truth to them. They wouldn't believe or they'd think you're crazy. The truth won't help the child."

"Whatever you say, Father."

"I'll be Anthony Novak's godfather. You've never been a father and I've never been a godfather. We'll learn together."

For the first time the man smiled. For a few moments, they stood close together as the priest anointed the sleeping child and intoned the prayers.

"I can see that he likes me already," said the priest,

handing the child to the man and walking to the book in which baptisms were registered.

"When's his birthday, Frank?"

"The landlady said that my wife told her the child was two in August."

"When in August?"

"Just August."

"As a godfather, I have some rights. And it's fitting that I give my godson a gift. I'm giving him my birthday, August fourth."

"Thank you, Father. Thank you very much."

"Not yet. Don't go yet."

"What is it, Father?"

"I want to speak to you as a friend for fifteen years, as your priest, and as one man to another."

"Yes, Father."

"Frank, if this doesn't work out . . . if you find that you cannot love this human being after all, tell me. Tell me and I'll understand. Please don't sentence yourself to years of sacrifice because of what you call duty."

"I'll tell you. I promise I will."

"Another thing. He's yours temporarily, Frank. Understand that. If you neglect him or mistreat him—no matter how—I will take him from you. He's my only godson. I'll take him!"

"If I fail, I'd want you to take him."

"Frank," the priest said, returning to his own cheerful nature, "I hope that someday you and I can sit down together and drink a few bottles of beer. My front door will always be open."

"As mine will be to you."

Frank had quit his job and had bought from the widow Bartek the shop on Fiftieth Street. It had been Bartek's tailor shop until the man had died of flu epidemic. Before

Bartek had made it into a tailor shop, Hruby the cobbler owned it. He had died there over his lasts, a very old man. No one could recall who had owned the place before Hruby. Frank had changed the building completely. He had cut it almost in half, making the back part into one large room that served as kitchen, parlor, and bedroom. He had built onto it an addition which was their bathroom. In the front of the store, he fashioned the fixit shop. That became his solution to the problem of looking after the child while earning a living for both of them.

In the front of the store, Frank fixed the clocks, the washing machines, the sewing machines, lamps, electric irons, or anything that needed fixing. He was a particular, unique kind of genius whose fingers had been made to think with tools in them. Patience, exquisite patience, was his. He repaired cars if they could be brought to his shop. Many of the factories called on him to repair or rebuild their machinery. When Frank went out on jobs, he took the child with him, strapped to his back with a harness he had made.

Frank never really had prospered, but he had managed to keep a comfortable home. Then came the Great Depression. Unemployment hit the city like a plague. The factories closed down. Money was scarce, and although Frank's services were needed more than at any other time, few people could pay him. Ironically, when jobs were good and paid good wages, people threw out the things that didn't work, but when paychecks were few and far between, they wanted their household items repaired but could pay very little for the services.

All during those lean, hard years, Frank kept the neighborhood's plumbing in good order. He fixed the stoves and space heaters. He kept clocks and washing machines going. He probably made the greatest contribution of all by keeping the children in warm clothing through his persistent efforts in maintaining the many treadle sewing machines.

It had been the priest's idea to spread the story that Frank was the boy's uncle. He had told everyone who asked that Frank's brother and his brother's wife had died of diphtheria someplace on the plains of Kansas. The story was accepted willingly and because people are that way, they gave to the boy their utmost in sympathy while seeing in the man everything that personified the fictional stepfather. To the priest's way of thinking, Frank seemed to earn more abuse than he was entitled to.

How much did the Baba really know, he wondered. Did she know, for instance, that Frank had no real legal claim to the boy?

3

How, the boy wondered, could his uncle remain so calm? How could he be so unconcerned. Here was a shoe box filled with five- and ten-dollar bills, and he wasn't even going to count it.

"Aren't you happy with what the Little People left for me?" Sonny asked, being a bit worried about his uncle's lack of enthusiasm.

"Of course I am pleased. I just don't know what to say."

"Say wowie, or something."

"Once there lived a man," said the uncle, beginning what the boy knew to be a story.

"In the old country or here?" Sonny teased.

"Which would you prefer?"

"Make it the old country."

"Good!" said the uncle. "Because that's where it happened."

"I don't think that it really happened. I think that you make up all of your stories as you go along."

The uncle chuckled, "This boy of mine—I've got to get rid of him. I thought of drowning him many times, but that would only pollute the lake."

"Go on with the story," Sonny begged impatiently.

"This man—he lived in Pilsen and if he lives yet, he is an old, old man but a very wise one—was a poor scholar. He lived in a cold attic room with his books, studying the philosophies of the world."

"Cats? Did he have cats? Many scholars keep cats."

"No cats. He was too poor to keep a cat. Whenever he acquired any money he bought books."

"Did he work? How did he get money?"

"Other scholars and some students came to him for instructions. Some brought him food and some paid him a few pennies for each lecture. They came to listen to his explanation of the mysterious philosophies of the orient."

"Why him? Why would they come to hear him?"

"Because he could read all of those strange languages. He could read Greek, Persian, Hindi, Chinese, and maybe even English."

Sonny was giggling, appreciating the uncle's sly humor.

"He must have been a smart man," Sonny concluded, "especially learning how to read English."

"He was smart, but poor. He studied and studied, hoping that one day he would make a great discovery which would bring him wealth and fortune."

"What kind of discovery could he make from reading?"

"There are such things as diamonds and rubies and emeralds and, of course, gold. Where do they come from? How are they made? Do you know?"

"No."

"Neither did our scholar. But he thought he could find out. He thought he might find one part of the mystery in the writings of the Chinese, more in the writings of the ancient Persians, and a little more in the written legends of the Norsemen. If he could spot the clues and put them together, he could very possibly have the answer."

"Supposing that he did? Supposing that he did make such a discovery, what could a poor scholar do with it?"

"He'd take it to his king, of course. What king would not make him a prince for such a discovery?"

"And did he make such a discovery?"

"Yes. He made a great discovery. Not about gold and jewels, but about something nearly as precious."

"What?"

"You're getting ahead of the story."

"All right. Have it your way."

"As you know, three fine rivers come together at Pilsen," the uncle began.

"How would I know?"

The story telling was another game which the boy and the uncle had developed together, and frequent interruptions were one of the rules the two had seemingly agreed upon a long time ago.

"I have just told you that three fine rivers come together at Pilsen. So, therefore, you know. And now you know that each river begins high in the Bohemian Forest, which makes the waters clear and cold. Three small rivers flow into Pilsen and one greater river flows out of Pilsen. The bigger river flows north and east toward Prague, although it doesn't enter the city."

"I know!" Sonny said in mock triumph. "This is a geography lesson and not really a story."

"I tell you all of these facts because they are important to a full and complete understanding of the story."

"Okay. Three fine rivers flow into Pilsen. . . ."

"Our scholar frequently fished in those three fine, cool, and clear rivers. Not that he liked fish, because he really didn't. But fish was a food that he did not need to buy with money. The price of the fish was only his time. And not much time either. Being a reader and a thinker, he could read while he fished and think on the way to and from the rivers. While he fished, he studied his books and charts, interrupting his work only to pull in a fish or bait his hook."

"A name! Did the scholar have a name?"

"Yes. He was called Master Holomecz. If he had a first name—which he probably did—no one knew it.

"So one fine morning our Master Holomecz took his books and his fishing pole to the banks of the Uhlava River, which was his favorite river of the three fine rivers flowing into Pilsen. With him he always took a small trowel. And this was for digging worms for bait. When our scholar got to his favorite spot on the river under a huge oak tree, he put the trowel to work. But no worms could he dig up. He looked on all the bushes for a caterpillar. None could he find. Frantically, he looked and looked for anything that moved or wiggled with which to bait his hook. Alas, nothing."

Sonny suggested, "He should have had some of your dumplings."

"Poor man," sighed the uncle. "He seldom had dumplings for his own food. And when he was lucky enough to feast on dumplings, not a morsel could he spare for bait. But this young man had a brain. After all, he was a great thinker. So what did he do? He searched his person for some article which might attract a bass or a trout. Perhaps a brightly colored button would work. Maybe the buckle from his shoe. A piece of his red underwear? What? What could he use for bait? He had not had breakfast that morning and his hunger was making him almost panic.

"Sometimes hunger and want drive people into doing fantastic things. We know that desperation has fathered many wonderful inventions. So while his mind raced through a catalog of the things on his person, he thought of the silver medal the university had given him as a token of his scholarship. It was small. Perhaps I should say that it was tiny. But whether it was small or tiny, it was oval shaped, and it was shiny. On the medal was the image of St. Thomas Aquinas, the patron saint of many scholars.

"In his desperation and with a prayer of apology to St. Thomas, the scholar tied the medal to the ring of the hook. No sooner had he thrown his line into the stream and dangled the bait than he had a strike. He pulled out of the stream the biggest trout in the kingdom. Back went St. Thomas on the hook and out came another huge trout. In less time than it takes to tell, he had caught seven of the finest trout ever seen by mankind.

"When our scholar went into the city, everyone was amazed at his magnificent catch. He traded one trout to the baker for a large loaf of bread. Another went to the tavern keeper for a bottle of fine wine. Two he sold to the banker for a crown each. The fifth one he gave to the mayor just to show the townspeople how generous he could be. The other two he took home and ate with great delight.

"Every day thereafter, he went to one of the three cool, clear rivers, tossed in his wonderful artificial bait, and hauled in the most magnificent trout or bass that God had put into those waters. He had no trouble selling his fish. People waited for him to enter the city with his catch. The bishop even became one of his best customers. And on Fridays, people placed their orders. 'Catch for me a large trout, Master Holomecz, please,' the banker would say. 'Bring whatever you catch to me,' the tavern keeper would say. 'I shall have as many patrons to dinner tonight as the number of fish you bring.'

"Now people being like they are, being always jealous of another's success, they all wanted to know what his secret was. They pestered him to know the kind of bait he used or if he used some kind of magic incantation. Some people suspected that he had made a secret pact with the devil and wanted to learn how they could make one too.

"One of the truths of life is that success is its own curse. Everyone felt that he should have a share in Holomecz's secret. Because the baker had given the scholar some crusts of stale bread, he thought that he was entitled to share in the scholar's secret. Everyone suddenly thought of hundreds of ways in which they had assisted the scholar when the poor fellow needed help the most. But Holomecz kept his lips sealed. At first he tried to tell the people that the fish he brought in were simply caught by fisherman's luck. But when they refused to accept that explanation, he sealed his lips and remained silent. He would not even share his secret with the poor parish priest who had gone fishing with him many times in the past.

"Poor Holomecz had no peace. If he were to walk through the city with his fishing pole, a crowd would soon gather and follow him. At times when he was successful in evading the crowds, he found many of his friends hiding in the bushes, hoping to spy on him. Once the tavern keeper even filled him with free beer, thinking that the scholar might let the secret slip out in a drunken conversation. Most of the other people simply nagged him.

"'Tell *me*, friend Holomecz,' they pleaded. 'With me your secret is safe.'

"The townspeople hounded him and dogged his tracks. Once he had found that someone had even broken into his little room and had searched it in case he had written down his secret. But Holomecz was very clever. He hid his secret where everyone could see it!"

The boy laughed. "How can anything which can be seen be hidden?"

"That's how Holomecz was so clever. He knew that the safest hiding place was no hiding place."

"I don't believe it," said the boy. "If I were to sit on the Public Square with a lapful of five- and ten-dollar bills, every bum in the city would be on me like the pigeons on the statue of Tom L. Johnson."

The uncle wagged his head impatiently. "I can see that you're not the scholarly type. The idea is to hide it openly. You conceal it where everyone can see it."

"All right, how?"

"Master Holomecz wore it in his hat. He slipped the hook into his hatband and let the medal hang free. Then he wound the fish line around and around and around. Everyone who saw the hat—and who didn't see it?— thought that the line was a decoration. And why shouldn't a scholar wear a medal of St. Thomas in his hat?"

The uncle jerked his hook out of the water and checked the bait. The piece of dumpling was still on it, so he threw it back. He remained silent for a long, long time, bobbing the hook up and down slowly. The boy soon found the silence intolerable.

"Well?" he asked.

"Well, what?" responded the uncle.

"Aren't you going on with the story?"

"Which story?"

"Come on, Unk!" the boy laughingly pleaded. This apparent abandonment of the story in the middle of it was also a part of the story game. "What happened to our scholar?"

"Oh, him?"

"Yes, him. What happened to Master Holomecz?"

"His life was miserable."

"You've already said that."

"That fact bears repeating," the uncle replied. "He was worse off than he was before. Now he couldn't even feed himself on the free fish in the stream. You might say that

he was even poorer than he was before. There was nothing
for him to do but to sell his discovery. He could sell the
secret to the highest bidder and let the new owner fight off
the crowds. But who? Who would pay a price for it? Who
would pay the most for the exclusive rights to his magic
hook? Who would be in a position to protect that exclusive
right once he bought it? The bishop?

"Then Master Holomecz had a brilliant idea: the king.

"Everyone knew that the king of Bohemia was a great
hunter and fisherman. Master Holomecz figured that if he
were to offer the magic hook to the king as a special gift,
the king in turn would reward him splendidly. Perhaps the
king would confer a special title upon him. Maybe he
would be appointed a special adviser to the king on fishing.
There was no telling what a grateful king might do to
reward such a faithful and generous subject.

"Therefore, with the magic hook in his hatband, Holomecz took the road going north out of Pilsen. The road
followed the river which was made up of the three cool,
clear streams which entered the other side of the city. At
first a whole mob of fishermen followed after him, thinking
that he intended to fish the big river. It wasn't until after
the sun had passed from east to west that some of them
began to drop out of the march and return to their regular
duties. Those who still clung to his heels frequently asked
him where he was going. But Holomecz maintained a
strict silence and a steady pace. Finally, the last of them
returned to the city. Master Holomecz rested on the banks
of the river and put his magic hook to work. Right off, he
caught a fine bass which he cooked immediately. Then he
returned to the road and walked until sunset. He caught
a fine trout for his dinner and went to sleep quite pleased
with himself. Before sleep overtook him, he had time to

turn over in his mind the many possible rewards the king might grant him.

"The next day passed much the same as the first, except that he had the road to himself. He had fresh bass for breakfast, lunch, and dinner. For a while, he thought that he might travel the world, living on fish, and studying the ways of the many peoples on earth. But his feet were his biggest weakness. He was one of those men who had a strong mind but weak feet.

"On the third day it rained, and poor Holomecz got drenched. But that night he was lucky enough to exchange a fine string of bass for a night's lodging at an inn in a tiny village. 'Never,' said the innkeeper, 'have I seen such fine bass.' And the taste so tickled his palate and the palates of his guests that he gave the scholar all the fine beer he could drink.

"The next day about noon, Holomecz was attacked in a big wood by robbers. When they were satisfied that the poor scholar was without even the smallest coin in his purse, they thumped him soundly and left him. But his fortune was still in his hat. So Holomecz picked himself up cheerfully, brushed off the bigger clods of dirt clinging to his clothes, and continued his journey. Again he had fish for every meal of the day, and perhaps because fish is brain food, Holomecz began to think of ways in which he could work for himself the best deal with the king. Maybe he could convince the king that the hook alone would not catch fish but needed a very secret saying, spoken at the proper time. So Holomecz put his mind to work, devising different ways in which to increase his own importance and, thereby, his chances of success.

"Holomecz started out with a light heart on the fifth morning. He knew that he would be at the palace or at least in the city by nightfall. Either that night or early the next morning he would have his reward. Perhaps he might receive an endowment from the king to continue his studies. Certainly the king would see that such a scholar deserved a fine appointment.

"At about noon he was in the Modrany forest outside of Prague. It was there that the gods seemed to smile the brightest on our poor scholar. Grazing calmly at the edge of a beautiful lake was a handsome red horse. It had a bridle but no saddle. 'The stars are with me,' said the scholar to himself. 'I can ride to the palace and see the king before he has his supper. I may even be invited to eat with him. How lucky I am!'

"So saying, Master Holomecz mounted the horse and rode it out of the forest. No sooner had he entered the square in front of the king's palace than the people and soldiers fell on him with cries, 'A beggar rides the king's horse. Alas, the king must be dead!'

"The king's soldiers dragged poor Holomecz from the horse and pounded him and thumped him severely.

"'What have you done to our king, scoundrel?' they demanded.

"'Scoundrel I am not. Nor am I a beggar,' Holomecz protested. 'I am Master Holomecz, the scholar of Pilsen.'

"'Liar!' they replied. 'Look at you. Look at yourself, beggar. Robber!'

"And poor Holomecz did look at himself. His shoes were tattered after five days of walking. His clothes were muddy, torn, and horribly wrinkled from having been slept in, been rained upon, and been subjected to the abuse of the robbers. In fact, he looked like one of the worst beggars. And the soldiers began to drag him off to prison.

"'Wait!' demanded the scholar. 'I must see the king. I

have brought a valuable gift for him all the way from Pilsen. I must see the king!'

"'Indeed you have a gift for the king,' laughed the captain of the guard. 'You shall give the king his horse.'

"'But I must see him,' Holomecz begged.

"'You shall,' said the captain, 'when the king sentences you to be hanged.'

"The fuss went on until the soldiers who had gone to look for the king's body returned. The king was with them and in a fine rage.

"'Where,' he demanded, 'is that low-bred scoundrel who had the audacity to steal my horse?'

"Right there in the palace square, Holomecz was forced onto his knees in front of his king.

"'Your majesty,' Holomecz pleaded. 'I found the poor animal alone and unattended. Thinking the horse had been lost, I brought it to the city to help find its owner. When one is tired, one does not lead a horse. He rides it.'

"Said the king, 'I was fishing not a hundred paces from where the horse was grazing. You could not have looked very hard for the horse's rider.'

"'The truth is, Majesty, that I was so anxious to see your majesty that when I came upon the poor beast, I considered it a sign of good fortune. The horse meant that I could proceed more speedily on my mission.'

"The king, who was known for his keen ear for a joke, roared with laughter. 'He steals my horse and leaves me stranded four miles from my palace so that he could see me sooner. The man is a comedian!'

"'Sire, I beg of you. Let me explain. I didn't know it was your horse.'

"'Whose horse did you suppose it was?' the king chided, thinking to humor the man who was obviously mad.

"'I thought that I was rescuing a horse that had run away from its rider.'

"'You thought that the horse had run away from its rider? Did you think that it ran away from its saddle too?'

"Now the whole crowd was laughing with the king at the king's humorous interrogation. Mothers held up their children so that they could see a stupid fellow.

"'Please, your majesty. Let me explain. I am Holomecz the scholar of Pilsen. I am no horse thief. Just a poor scholar who has made a long journey to bring his gracious king a gift.'

"'We are back to the gift again,' the king announced. 'All right, scholar. Present your gift. Everyone knows me to be a patient man. So give me the gift before I hang you.'

"With renewed hope and thinking that he might not only save his life but also receive a reward from the king, Holomecz unwound the fish line and held his magic hook for the king to see.

"'What kind of nonsense is this?' demanded the king.

"'I call it my magic hook,' Holomecz explained eagerly. 'See the medal? It's an artificial bait. With this hook I catch the biggest trout and bass there are. No trout or bass can resist it.'

"The king laughed and laughed. The soldiers laughed and laughed. And the people who were twenty rows deep all around them laughed and laughed. When those who were the farthest back asked why everyone was laughing and were told about the artificial bait the scholar had brought all the way from Pilsen, they laughed too.

"'Truly the man is mad,' said the king mournfully. 'He expects me to believe that a fish would think that a medal of St. Thomas—may his name forever be praised!—was something to eat.'

"'He is a fool,' agreed the captain of the guard. 'Every

good fisherman knows that it's the odor of the bait that attracts the fish.'

"'Poor fellow!' lamented the king. 'His mind is gone. He's probably been studying too much.'

"'What should I do with him?' asked the captain. 'Should I throw him into the dungeon?'

"'Please, please, please, your majesty,' Holomecz begged in tears. 'Just let me demonstrate my magic hook.'

"Ignoring the poor man, the king said to his captain, 'No. He is a harmless fool. Feed him and turn him loose.'

"The king started to the palace and the soldiers were leading Holomecz to the guardroom where they would give him supper when the scholar broke free and ran after the king, shouting, 'My magic hook. You still have my magic hook. May I please have it back for it is the only way I can get food? Without it, I shall have to beg.'

"'No!' said the king. 'This devil's thing is probably the source of your madness. It is better that I destroy it. So go and get your supper before I change my mind and throw you in the dungeon after all.'"

There followed a pause during which Sonny patiently waited for his uncle to go on. When he could wait no longer, he asked, "So?"

"So, what?"

"What happened next?"

"I know no more of the story," said the uncle. "Holomecz was never seen or heard from again by any of his friends."

Sonny was silent for a while, and then he asked, "What does it mean?"

"What does what mean?"

Acting exasperated, Sonny explained, "What does the story mean?"

"I'm not sure that it has a meaning. It's just a story told

to pass the time away. My great-grandfather knew Holomecz and had heard about the tragedy. It was my great-grandfather who told the story to me when I was a small lad, sitting next to him on the banks of the Uhlava River, fishing."

"Come on now, Unk," the boy entreated. "You know that all of your stories mean something. They have to mean something or you don't tell them."

"A story," said the uncle, "is like a mixed stew. It tastes like whatever the eater thinks it tastes like."

"What you're saying is that I've got to figure it out for myself."

As if he hadn't heard the remark, the uncle asked, "Care for another piece of bread?"

4

Walking down Broadway toward his home, the priest was so lost in his thoughts that he failed to hear a car following alongside of him and failed to hear its driver calling his name. Getting ahead of the priest, the driver stopped the sedan, slid across its front seat, and planted himself on the sidewalk where the priest would either have to recognize him or walk over him.

"Hi, Doc," the priest said. "Where did you pop up from?"

"Can I give you a lift, Father?" Dr. Macek asked, pointing to the Franklin at the curb.

"No thanks, Vince," the priest refused. "I need the exercise. You yourself told me that I needed to get more exercise."

"Wait then," said the doctor. "I'll walk with you. There's nothing like a doctor taking his own advice."

The priest and Mopsy waited for the doctor to cut off the engine and pick up his black bag.

"I thought I'd have to run you down to get your attention," the doctor complained. "I'd say you're a man with a problem on his mind."

The priest replied with a grin, "I'd say that it's you with a mind full of something. Any time our good doctor abandons his car to walk with the parish priest, it's more than companionship that the doctor wants."

"Why, Father." The doctor acted surprised and shocked. "We're more than just friends. We're partners. You take care of the souls, and I look after the bodies. We're indispensable to each other, so why shouldn't we walk side by side?"

"Which means that you do not intend to invade my territory but wish to discuss somebody. Whose body?"

"I didn't think that I was that obvious," said the doctor by way of indicating that their meeting was not entirely accidental. "I have to talk to you about someone. But I was only trying to be casual and friendly. Trouble is that you have a suspicious mind."

"Is the mind a part of the body?" the priest challenged. "If you're not sure that it is, then you're invading my territory."

They both laughed at the banter as could two old friends who had debated and discussed together many issues and problems of the community. It was true that they were partners of a sort. Both were at every tragedy. The doctor and the priest appeared together at the bedside of the very ill. Both were at the scene of accidents and catastrophes. In all of the human sufferings in the neighborhood they were partners.

Not only were the two men in contrasting professions, their figures were as unlike as possible. The priest was smallish, very thin. The doctor was a big man. He had a broad back and a large stomach. He stood almost a full head above the priest.

"Seriously, Father," the doctor began, "I'm in a bind. One of our neighbors insists that I go with some kind of delegation to see about something I have no heart for."

"Don't go. That's all you have to do. Say you're too busy. For telling a little lie like that I'll give you a small penance."

"I've sloughed her off with that alibi already. Now she wants me to write or sign some document—a deposition lawyers call it. The piece of paper will take my place at the proposed hearing. And I don't want to do that either."

"Then don't. You're a doctor. You have the right to protect your patient, if that's what it's all about."

"That's just it. The whole thing is about protecting the health and safety of a patient."

"Just refuse," advised the priest, "if you don't think that it will be of any help to your patient."

"Fine. But what if the court calls me and asks me to present certain facts in the interest of the case. Can I refuse our courts? Can I give false testimony?"

"No. Of course not."

"You may not know it yet," the doctor warned, "but you're in the middle of it too. She has you in her plans."

The priest nodded, saying in a somber tone, "I already know about it. It's Sonny Novak, and it's the Baba causing the fuss. What's she after you for?"

"She claims that Frank has neglected the boy's health and wants me to testify to that."

"Fiddlesticks! My gosh, that boy has had the best of care. If I had to criticize Frank's care of the boy, I'd say that he's been too protective. How can she make such a claim or expect you to support it?"

"A couple of years ago, the boy had pneumonia. Remember? She claims that the pneumonia was the result of Frank's neglect. As you very well know, Father, we came very close to losing that boy."

"Yes, the boy got pneumonia. Many people get pneumonia. Many people get it and die from it. But with the grace of God and your skill, the boy lives today."

"Her claim is that had Frank provided for the boy properly, he wouldn't have caught it in the first place."

"Is that true? Scientifically true?"

"I can't argue against proper care as a preventative. The

disease is most likely to take over in a body that's been run-down."

"No one can expect Frank to control the weather. You remember that day. It was Good Friday, and it was a miserable day. Rain mixed with wet snow—a raw wet windy day."

"And the boy was running around in all that foul weather in tennis shoes and a light sweater. Our opponent claims that if the boy had been properly dressed, if he had had a raincoat and at least proper shoes, he'd not have come down with the disease."

The priest felt his temper rising, but he controlled it, saying, "I don't believe that the Baba would go this thing alone. She's not that smart nor all that brave. Who else is involved in this?"

"I thought you knew," said the doctor. "Maresh, the lawyer, is the one who called me."

"Oh, I see," responded the priest. "I heard that he's running for councilman for our ward to fill that vacancy."

"It was Maresh who called me about the deposition. Do you think I would have bothered with the old lady? For some strange reason, he's helping her."

"Vince, you can believe me that it was maybe more my fault that Sonny got sick that day than Frank's. And she was to blame too. It was my fault for taking Frank away from the shop the way that I did. And it was her fault for sending the boy out looking for him."

"I only know what I saw. I only know that when I got there, I found a very sick boy. I found soaking wet clothes on a chair and threadbare tennis shoes wringing wet. The room was as cold as an ice house. Frank was chopping up furniture, trying to get some heat into the place. I believe that it was you who brought a bag of coal. As I say, I only know what I saw, and that's all I can tell the court."

"Vince, it was all my fault. I was to blame and not Frank."

"If you mean to say that it's your fault for not being aware of their needs and failing to perform a few simple acts of charity, then I must share that blame with you. How many times have I seen that kid running down the street and waved to him without ever wondering if he'd had breakfast? When did I get concerned? When I walked into that room and found that he had pneumonia."

"No, no," said the priest bitterly. "I'm more directly involved. I took Frank away that day. You know the big cross above the altar with all the lights on it? Something happened and they wouldn't go on. I was going to have the Stations at three that afternoon and again at seven. And I wanted the cross to be lit. So I drove over and got Frank. Sonny was out making deliveries for Pasek. It was almost three, and I didn't give Frank even time to write a note telling Sonny where he'd gone. Frank got the lights going just in time for the services. But by then the storm had broken. Lightning, thunder, and pouring down wet, snowy rain. I hadn't even given Frank time to get a coat, so I made him stay until after the services so I could drive him home."

"So that's why there was no fire in the kitchen stove," said the doctor. "Frank must have been out all day, too."

"That's another way in which I was wrong. I was so concerned about my Good Friday services that I never thought to ask Frank if Sonny was all right or if they had something for the evening meal. I didn't even bother to ask Frank if he had other plans. I just insisted that he help me out. And you know Frank. He wouldn't yell fire if his britches were in flames."

"Still, Sonny was running around in that storm improperly dressed. And the way that I understand it, Sonny was wearing the best that he had."

"Frank would never have let the boy go out dressed like that," the priest insisted. "If Frank had been there, he wouldn't have let the boy go out. And if Frank had been there, the boy would have had no reason to go out."

"There's the fire," pointed out the doctor, "or I should say that there was no fire."

"How do we know what Frank had in mind? Can we say that Frank would have sat around all evening with that boy with no fire in the stove? Frank's an ingenious man. He has always provided for both of them before. How do we know what Frank had in his mind for heating the place? It was two o'clock when I grabbed him. All that I can remember is that I found him in his shop. He must have been working on some job. For all we know he may have had money in his pocket or money promised to him. He *could* have gone out and bought a couple of bags of coal if I hadn't dragged him off with me."

"It all sounds like a game of 'if.' *If* such and such had not happened and *if* so and so had done such and such. I'm only the poor doctor who treated the unfortunate patient. I wish the old battle-ax would leave me out of this."

"That's the hard part—the part that sends my temper soaring. It was the widow Hronek who drove the boy out into the storm. She came to Frank's shop practically in hysterics. Sonny was home before the storm had broken. Maybe there was no fire in the stove, but he had a roof over his head. She came bustling into the place, demanding Frank. Her kitchen was flooding! Everything would be ruined! She probably scared the daylights out of the poor boy. What could Sonny do? He could stay there while the old lady had fits or he could go out looking for his uncle.

Which would you do? Sonny took the easy way out. He went looking for his uncle and got caught in the world's worst storm."

The doctor had to laugh in spite of himself. "So why blame yourself?"

"I get mad at myself for not teaching the boy how to defend himself against hysterical women."

Increasing his laughter, the doctor said, "Father, if you know any secret defense like that, please tell me. Had the widow come to me with a busted hot water tank in the kitchen, I too would have run out into a tornado to look for help rather than sit and listen to her carry on."

"Sonny should have stayed where he was no matter what. He went out looking for Frank. He was out in that storm for more than an hour. And when he finally thought of checking the church, Frank and I had gone already. He walked home in that awful storm."

"And when he got home," the doctor suggested, "I suppose that Frank had left again for the widow's place?"

"Exactly. But this time he left a note."

"That's when the boy could have used the heat. He must have been drenched clean through. But what was Frank thinking about?"

"Of course I didn't go in with Frank. I just dropped him off at the front door. You can bet that the widow never told Frank that Sonny had gone out to look for him. She knew better. If Frank had known that Sonny was out in that storm, he would have let the widow's kitchen become a river. And she knew it!"

Without fully realizing it, the two men had come to the priest's house, had turned up the walk, gone up the steps, across the porch, and into the parlor. Mopsy, who had remained at her master's heels all during the walk home, broke her obedient pace once the door was opened and dashed with her package into the kitchen.

"Worst of all," continued the priest, "I forgot to pay Frank. I keep thinking that had I offered him a few dollars, he might have had me stop at Bican's coal yard to pick up a few bags of fuel."

Unceremoniously, the two had taken chairs in the cool parlor. The doctor had removed his bowler hat and placed it on top of his black bag which he set on the floor next to his chair. In the kitchen, Mopsy could be heard wrestling with the wrapped bag of bones. For her, part of the fun of bones was having to fight the wrapping paper.

"Frank wouldn't have asked you to do him a favor even if his life had depended upon it," was the doctor's considered opinion. "Even if you had paid him, he wouldn't have done anything with it. You know that he went directly to the widow's house to fix that blasted tank!"

The room and the house was quiet except for Mopsy. The priest broke into their separate thoughts by suggesting, "Coffee? The woman next door, my housekeeper, pops in and out all day to keep me in coffee and make sure that I eat lunch and dinner."

Without waiting for a reply, the priest went into the kitchen, rattled and banged, and returned with two mugs of steaming coffee between which, on a tray, was a bottle of cream. The doctor waved off the cream, preferring his coffee strong and black. The priest liked his half cream and half coffee. Silently, without comment as it befits old friends, the priest presented to the doctor an open box of long, thin cigars. They both took one, nipped off the ends, and puffed the room full of blue smoke. They sipped their coffee and puffed on their cigars, enjoying both pleasures immensely. Even the most casual observer would have noticed that this ritual was one the two had enjoyed together many times.

"It was about seven o'clock that evening when Frank came for me," the doctor recalled. "I was out on a case at the hospital, but I went right over as soon as I came in. Frank must have missed me by no more than fifteen minutes."

Shaking his head sadly at his recollections, he continued, "The boy was shivering and burning up with fever. Frank was knocking apart a footstool and stuffing it into the kitchen stove. He was soaking wet too, probably from the run to my house and back. I kept nagging at him to warm up the place. With his bare hands he tore a kitchen chair apart and stuffed it into the stove. Then he went after that little oak table that the lamp rested on by his bed. He couldn't break that with his hands, so he stomped it apart. Like a mad man, he was furious. I had to leave the boy and talk to him. He had the stove almost red hot, and he was sizing up the kitchen table. More to give him something to do than anything else, I sent him for you. I felt sure that we would need you before the night was out, so I sent him then."

Again there was a silence as each man relived that awful night. Finally, the priest asked, "Can you really say that it was neglect? After what you know now, can you in all good conscience say that Frank was guilty of neglect?"

"No, not neglect," said the doctor. "That evening I learned a new lesson in a man's devotion to a boy. And I saw something else too. I saw a priest I have known for a long time almost go to pieces over the same boy."

"That's our secret, Vince. No one must ever know that part of the story."

"Funny thing about being a doctor—you find out very quickly who really cares about whom.

"When and if Lawyer Maresh asks me, I shall have to tell him that Sonny got a bad break. He was the victim of a nasty arrangement of coincidences," the doctor continued.

"Thanks, Vince," said the priest. "Thanks for checking into things. You don't know how important it is to me."

"Maybe I shouldn't know," said the doctor. "Maybe I already know too much or have seen too much."

"I'll tell you this," said the priest. "The circumstances around Sonny's being in Frank's care can't be examined too closely. If somebody gets to prying around, they may find something that will hurt Sonny more than it will help him."

"Say no more. The less I know about the case, the better I will feel. I can only say with deep conviction that Frank did the best he possibly could for the boy."

Picking up his black bag and his hat, the doctor started for the door but paused to say, "The court might accept the pneumonia as something that could have happened to anyone. But what if someone from downtown comes poking around and looks into Sonny's wardrobe? What if someone checks into Frank's food supplies? The court just might be concerned more with the future than the past."

"Don't worry about that," said the priest. "Frank has always provided for the boy. Maybe not the best, but you can be sure that Sonny has never gone hungry."

The doctor shrugged happily. "If we don't have to worry about that, what do we have to worry about? We've got no problems. The woman hasn't got a case."

"Sure," said the priest. "We're worrying about nothing. Now if Sonny were to break into a bank or rob a jewelry store, then we'd have worries."

"Now don't forget this," said the doctor sternly. "If you need a couple of bucks to help fill the coal shed or to get the kid some new clothes, let me know. I might not be the most successful doctor in the city when it comes to my bank account, but I'll always have a few extra dollars for Frank and the boy."

"Thanks," said the priest. "But you know Frank. He won't accept charity. He wants to make it on his own. And I guess the boy feels the same way."

"That's all okay with me, but you may have to take charge a little bit. Maybe you ought to tell Frank that someone is trying to cause him trouble. Maybe you ought to talk to him like a brother rather than a priest."

"Frank's not the man you can talk to like a priest or a brother or a doctor, as a matter of fact. And you know that!"

"Good luck to all of you."

Standing on the porch, the doctor added, "That woman! She got me all excited over nothing. And I'm not the excitable type. Just wait until she comes to me with one of her belly aches. A double dose of castor oil for her. Will I fix her!"

With a wave of his hand, the doctor strode down the porch steps and went up the street in search of his car. The priest went into the kitchen and poured himself another cup of coffee. Sitting at the kitchen table, he sipped the hot brew slowly, thoughtfully. He thought he should feel elated over the way he had handled the crisis, and he wondered why he wasn't. His mind kept returning to that Sunday when he had baptized the boy. Frank had no real claim to the child. There were no real blood ties. The priest wondered if the police in Chicago had known this. What if someone were to go to Kansas and search out Sonny's invented parents? The solution suddenly became apparent: there must never be a reason for anyone to search into the boy's past.

5

The sun was at its highest point. The beach was filling up with people, mostly with mothers and their young children. Already some of the young teen-agers were gathering. Girls and boys were arriving in separate groups. One group of boys had a ball and had begun a game of catch, choosing a spot especially close to where a group of girls had arranged themselves on a blanket. On several occasions the ball invaded the territory claimed by the girls, and the girls protested vigorously. Finally the boys had given up their game, and the girls were kind enough to share their blanket with the boys.

The rocks, too, were beginning to get crowded. Many men, made idle by the Depression, took up fishing more to use time than to add provender to their tables. The men on the rocks talked and fished. The women on the beach talked and scolded the children. And the teens talked and teased each other.

Crowds seemed to make Frank uncomfortable. Perhaps it was because he really wasn't a good talker. Frank indicated to Sonny that he was ready to go by picking up the mushrooms and putting them into an old salt bag he always carried. The fishing gear, the sack of mushrooms, the canteen, and even the fish went into the knapsack. Fitting the pack to his shoulders, he waited for the boy to adjust his own. The outline of the shoe box in the boy's pack was clearly visible.

Following the lake's shore eastward, the two headed

toward the river and the docks where coal and iron ore were loaded and unloaded from giant lake freighters. They then turned southward, following in the general direction of the crooked river. Here were all kinds of docks and freight terminals. A shorter walk home would have been over the bridge and through the downtown section of the city, but they never took that route. Uncle Frank's excuse was that the city streets of commerce were not very interesting. Sonny's interpretation of that was that the city streets of commerce were kept clean whereas the roads in the Flats frequently held the kind of findings his uncle was interested in. Sonny felt the same way. He would rather walk along the railroad tracks than on sidewalks. He had noticed a long time ago that when he and his uncle walked the city streets with knapsacks, people stopped and stared at them as if they were hobos.

Sonny balanced himself on a rail and walked it while the uncle paced his strides with the ties. When he came upon a large lump of coal, he picked it up and put it into a gunny sack he drew from the knapsack. Spying another lump of coal next to the tracks, he popped it in with the first.

"Unk, forget about picking up coal. I'm going to buy you one of those new gas space heaters for your shop."

"The coal is free from the Little People, and the stove in the shop is already paid for."

"You said that the money I found might belong to someone. What about the coal?"

"What about it?"

"Doesn't the coal you find belong to someone? The railroad maybe?"

"That's different."

"How different? The railroad buys the coal to run its trains. Then it owns the coal."

"A lump of coal falls from a train. Another falls and still another. The railroad thinks in terms of tons. It cannot be bothered with lumps, so it abandons them. I salvage the spill-off and give the abandoned little lumps a happy home."

"Might not the money have been abandoned?"

"Perhaps. By someone who is insane."

"Some nut has millions and millions of dollars. He thinks in terms of millions and abandons a few thousand here and there. I pick up the spill-off and give it a home. What's wrong with that?"

"It's a good story, but I find it difficult to believe."

"Finders keepers; losers weepers," the boy sang.

They left the tracks to walk on Canal Road. Stretching upward high above them was the Terminal Tower. On their level were the tracks which took the passenger trains in and out of the terminal. Only electric engines ran on those tracks. Sonny stopped to watch a train pull out and head east. Some of the passengers in the day coaches waved to him.

"Wouldn't you like to take a trip, Unk?"

"Where?"

"Anyplace. Do you have any more family? You could go visiting."

"I've got all the family I need right here. Maybe one too many."

"I must be your richest relative," the boy said triumphantly.

They waited for a tug pulling a barge to go through a bascule bridge and then crossed the river. The boy tried to spit into the river through the grating in the roadway without losing step with his uncle. On the fourth try he did it. They were once again on the west side of the river. At the steel wire mill, three of its six stacks were smoking. About a week earlier, only one stack, or one open-hearth furnace, had been in operation. Frank wondered if he could take it as a sign that things were getting better or if the smoke meant that the mill was working on its stacks.

The uncle spied a piece of steel lying in the road. Into his gunny sack it went.

"What did you find now?" asked the boy, who was dragging a stick along the chain link fence around the factory.

"The broken leaf of a truck spring."

"What good is it? Not even the truck wanted it."

"There's good steel in a truck spring. Who can tell when I'll need a piece just like it?"

"I'm going to buy you a truck, Unk. That's what I'll do. I'll paint your name on it, and you can go all over the city fixing things. You already have enough spare parts in the shop to fix every blooming thing in Cleveland."

When the uncle made no reply, the boy continued his tease, "Frank Novak and Company the truck will read. I'll be the company and you can do the work."

"I'm glad that you didn't think you could be my helper."

"Why?"

"I've known many people with five thumbs on each hand, but you're the only one who has five toes on each hand."

"That's all right, Unk. I'll work with my brain."

"That means you'll be unemployed."

"Go ahead and laugh. I'll make you famous."

"How?"

"Through advertising. I'll get you the truck and I'll advertise. There's no one else like you in the city."

"That's why I'm so rich."

"The trouble with you is that when you fix something, it never needs to be fixed again. You've already fixed everything in our neighborhood once. So there's nothing left for you to do but branch out."

"Wouldn't it be a lot easier to just move the shop? Fix everything in one neighborhood and move on?"

"I like the truck idea better," was the boy's opinion. "We could use the truck on Wednesdays and Sundays to go fishing."

"Anything you say," the uncle laughed. "After all, you're the brains of the outfit."

The Cuyahoga River twists through a deep valley that averages about a half-mile wide. Huge bridges span this gorge at many places. One such bridge connects the main thoroughfares of Lorain and Carnegie. Sonny stood under it and gazed upward at the roadway almost a hundred feet over his head. Tires, speeding over the concrete, created a hum which grew louder and diminished with the approach and passing of each vehicle. Sonny listened thoughtfully for a while. Then he ran to catch up with his uncle.

"I'd like to own that bridge," he announced.

"Why?"

"I'd put me a chair on one end and charge a dime for every car that goes across."

"Day and night?" asked the uncle.

"What?"

"Would you sit there day and night to collect your dimes?"

"I'd close it except for certain hours. Just during the few seconds I stood there, I counted twelve cars. That would be a buck twenty. I could close my bridge and quit for the day right now."

"How would you come upon the ownership of such a fine bridge? Would you buy it with the money you have in the shoe box?"

The boy laughed. "I might. Then again, I might buy me some other bridge. Maybe that bascule bridge down the river I'd buy. When I got tired of collecting dimes, I'd just open it and leave it. Cars couldn't use it until I felt like putting the bridge down again. I might buy it just for a toy to play with. Toot, toot! Up, up, up goes the bridge. Toot! Down it goes. Here comes a boat. I open the bridge if the captain is my friend. Or maybe I just won't open it. Let all the boats wait. It's my bridge. It would depend upon how I would feel. I could have a lot of fun with a bridge like that."

As Sonny spoke of the bascule bridge, he demonstrated the opening and closing of it with his hands across his chest, finger tips to finger tips. Then he thought of a swing bridge and performed that operation by swinging from his waist with hands outstretched.

"Here's a jackknife bridge," he said, standing on his toes and swinging his arms from an outstretched position to a point over his head.

"I'm going to be a bridge builder," Sonny announced. "Someday I will be building bridges all over the world. Big, beautiful bridges."

"And charge people to cross them?"

"I don't know." Sonny became serious. "The trouble is that if I have to collect, then I can't go out and build more. I think that I'll build them and sell them. Or I'll build them for someone who wants to sit in a chair and collect. The first one I build, I'll give to you."

"Do you know what it takes to be a bridge engineer?"

"Money. Everything takes money."

"Besides that?"

Sonny sighed sadly, "Oh, I suppose that I'd have to go to school for a long time. Why is it that everything good that you want to do makes you go to school for a long time?"

Without slowing his pace, the uncle bent forward and scooped up a length of steel chain lying in the road. He counted five full links. It looked like the chain might have fallen off a gasoline truck.

"School is the most efficient way to get a lot of knowledge quickly."

"I'd rather go to work for a bridge builder and learn from the job."

"So you put up your first bridge and right away it collapses. You say to yourself, 'I guess that's the wrong kind of bridge; I'll try a different kind this time.' Remind me not to walk on any of your bridges."

"I might not let you walk on any of my bridges. You may stamp on them purposely to make them fall."

"You'd have to pay me to go across one of your bridges. I wouldn't take a chance like that for nothing. I'm not going to walk on any bridges built by amateurs."

They had crossed another bridge and were back on the east side of the river. They were on the meandering street called Broadway. Oil refineries were to their left. Sonny didn't have to look at them. He knew that they were there by the odor. The day was becoming hot and muggy and the smoke and gaseous odors settled in the valley. Sonny could practically taste the refineries and his eyes smarted.

"Just because a guy goes to school it doesn't mean that he's smart," Sonny stated.

"Perhaps."

"Take Holomecz, the scholar. He was stupid."

"Oh?"

"He had a big chance, and he muffed it."

"How so?"

"If he had looked for the rider of the horse, whom would he have found?"

"The king."

"Right! He would have found the king sitting by the lake, fishing. Now, if I had been Holomecz, I would have sat next to the king just like he was an ordinary fisherman. I would have unwound my line and thrown out my magic hook. I'd let the king's eyes pop out. After I had pulled in a couple of big bass, the king would have been begging me for the hook."

"How would you have known that the fisherman was the king?"

"I'd know. Anyone would know. Anyone riding a horse like that had to be somebody."

"And so Holomecz was guilty of being stupid?"

"Sure. He had the best chance in the world to show the king what the hook would do, and he muffed it. Sheer stupidity!"

"Maybe," the uncle slyly suggested, "his sore feet were complaining so much that when he saw the horse he thought with the wrong end of his body."

"If he had been a real scholar, he would have used his head. He would have thought it out. I would have."

"Isn't that the whole idea of education? You learn what mistakes not to make. You learn about the bridges that have fallen down as well as those that have been standing for hundreds of years. Right now you know exactly what not to do if you should find a king's horse."

"You're doing it to me again, Unk," the boy complained mildly.

"What?"

"You know. You're pulling my leg."

The man placed the flat of his hand on the boy's head and ruffled his hair.

"Better the leg than a fistful of hair," he chuckled.

The two continued on in a companionable silence. Twice the boy drifted into the weeds along the far side of the road to check on beverage bottles. The quart-sized ginger ale and root beer bottles carried a five-cent deposit on them. He could trade one such empty bottle in for an ice cream bar. The first bottle was cracked. The second one was a liquor bottle. He was a bit disappointed. He would have liked to have found two such bottles for he was sure that his uncle would have enjoyed an ice cream bar too on such a hot afternoon.

They must have been walking for more than an hour, and the day was getting hotter. Sonny could see that the back of his uncle's shirt was soaking wet. He knew that his must also be in the same condition. Neither of them on any of their hikes had ever complained about either the heat or the cold or even the rain. They always seemed to accept the weather for what it was. They neither wished for a more favorable weather nor did they express regret for the day being what it was. It was as if they had long ago reached an agreement never to discuss the weather.

Frank sat on the grassy slope of a hill, removed his knapsack, and took out the canteen. First he offered it to the boy who, with a wave, indicated that his uncle should drink first. After the old man had drunk, the boy accepted it. While the boy drank, the uncle mopped his brow and face with a huge square of clean cloth that served as his handkerchief. With the canteen back in the pack, the uncle harnessed up again, and the two started off once more.

"That's what your story meant, though. Wasn't it?" asked the boy.

"Wasn't what?"

"Unk! You're doing it again."

"Doing what?"

"Pulling my leg."

"I'm only trying very hard to understand what you're talking about."

"The story of Holomecz—it means to think with your head and not with your feet."

"The one who has a taste for cabbage usually thinks that he eats cabbage stew."

"Unk! You're absolutely, gigantically impossible!"

"I may be improbable, yes. But certainly not impossible. Because you can see me and because you speak to me, I must exist."

"Now you're playing games with words," the boy accused.

"I'm only trying to point out a simple truth, that's all."

"You're kicking my question around. That's what you're doing. You're trying not to answer it."

"Which question are we talking about now?"

"The question is, teacher: Does your story of Holomecz mean that a man must learn to think with his head?"

"And I have said that a story means to the listener whatever the listener wants it to mean."

"Which is your way of saying that I haven't got it yet."

"Got what?"

"I haven't got the answer to your riddle or the solution to your parable. This dumb look I have comes from living with you. I'm not really that dumb. I know you and your parables. You always spring one on me when you're trying to get me to learn something. It's your way."

"Is it? Really?"

"Yes, really. With your parables you should have been a priest. You could come up with a different one every Sunday and never have to repeat yourself."

"You make me wiser than I am," the uncle protested.

"My stories are stories told for the entertainment of my young companion in life."

"And if the stories happen to be instructional, it's purely an accident."

"Right!"

"Then it means that I have not yet found the lesson in the Holomecz parable. But I'll keep looking."

No sidewalks were in that part of the Flats. The uncle walked along a dirt path between a pair of railroad tracks and the curb of the paved street. The boy walked the curb, swinging his hands to keep his balance. The uncle's long strides soon put him several yards ahead of the boy's short, tightrope-walking steps. As the boy watched his uncle lope along, he once again felt the sense of pride he had always felt in being with the man. His uncle always maintained an erect bearing. Although he was only of average height, his squared shoulders resting on a ramrod spine gave the impression that he was much taller than he was. The pack, which he always carried on his hikes, rested easily as if it were weightless. Sonny saw in his uncle's walk both pride and authority. The man, no matter how tired he might be, never slouched along. Sonny recalled a long, long time ago when his uncle began taking him on serious hikes. "Head up. Shoulders back. Look proud," the uncle had reminded him.

As Sonny watched his uncle march along, he imagined him wearing one of those fancy officer's uniforms which he had seen Douglas Fairbanks wear in movies about kings and soldiers. He always imagined his uncle as being a colonel or a major in the king's own guard.

Seeing his uncle, the colonel, break his stride to pick up a lump of coal the size of a goose egg jarred the image he had created in his mind. The uncle had scooped up the coal and had dropped it into the gunny sack swinging from his left hand. Perhaps it was the thought of a colonel in the king's own guard picking up coal that caused Sonny to be irritated. Perhaps Sonny felt embarrassed for this great man of dignity and bearing who had to pick coal along the railroad tracks.

"Leave it, Unk! It's too small to carry home."

"It's not too small. It's just the right size for the forge."

As the boy walked, his habit-trained, scavenger eyes swept the gutter in front of him. Shortly after the exchange on the small lump of coal, the boy spied a coin in the dirt along the curb. Picking it up, he flipped it in his hand several times, and then he flung it down the street.

"It's only a penny," he informed his uncle. "Who needs it?"

If the uncle was surprised or felt any dismay, he kept it to himself.

They started up Broadway hill toward Thirty-fourth Street. The boy walked behind the man with his hands against the man's pack, pretending to be pushing the man up the hill.

Thinking of his uncle as a colonel in the guard or perhaps as a soldier of fortune or some type of adventurer, the boy asked seriously, "Unk, what would you be if you didn't have me to look after?"

"Lonely," said the uncle.

"Oh, come on, Unk. You know what I mean. Would you be a wildcat oil prospector or a builder of bridges?"

"What makes you ask?"

"I just don't think you'd be doing what you are doing if it hadn't been for me."

"I'd be with Admiral Byrd at the South Pole."

"I knew it!"

"Or with Frank Buck in Borneo."

"Great!"

"Or married to the widow Hronek and raising a family of my own."

"I can't believe it. You married to Baba Chlepna? You couldn't stand her!" He was back-peddling up the hill, looking into his uncle's face.

"No worse than standing you for ten years."

Giving it up, the boy said, "I'll buy you that suit of armor and let you marry that princess."

They came to the fixit shop. The boy opened the front door. It wasn't locked; had never been locked. In the big kitchen, the uncle shed his knapsack as did the boy. Out came the mushrooms to be spread out on the breadboard. The boy took the gunny sack out the back door and to the coal shed. He came back with it, folded the empty sack, and tucked it back into his uncle's knapsack. Picking up the steel bar and the chain, he went into the workshop. The bar he stuffed into a bin holding other pieces of flat steel.

"What should I do with the chain?" he wanted to know.

"Hang it on that hook by the forge. You'll see some other links there."

When the boy returned to the kitchen, the uncle was cleaning the fish. The boy joined him. The boy then peeled a large potato. The shoe box, almost completely forgotten, lay on the boy's bed.

6

Having had lunch, the priest returned to his parlor where he tried to read the morning *Plain Dealer*. His mind refused to co-operate, so he let the newspaper fall to the floor. Walking over to the library table with the fringed lamp on it, standing in front of the parlor window, he opened the drawer and rummaged among paid household bills and very old greeting cards until he found the snapshot he was looking for. The picture had been taken by Frank with the priest's box camera. The scene was Nelson Ledges State Park where they had gone a long time ago on a Fourth of July outing. Standing in front of a huge boulder was the priest, and in his arms rested a small boy in rompers. On the back of the photo was written: "Sonny, Age 3."

More rummaging through the drawer uncovered Sonny's first holy communion picture. There sat the boy holding the missal the priest had given him. The priest clicked his tongue sadly. No one could say that the boy looked pious. In fact, there was an unmistakable glint of a pixy in his eyes. The priest admitted to himself that he wouldn't have been surprised if Sonny had had a toad or a turtle in his jacket pocket during the taking of the photo.

The priest was a bit sorry now that he hadn't taken more pictures of the boy. But that time when Sonny was so sick, he discovered that he had become more than just fond of the boy. He had decided then to withdraw as much as possible from the boy's life.

That terrible night more than two years ago came into his mind. Drenched and distraught, Frank had burst into the priest's home. The priest had just finished the Good Friday evening services and was in his kitchen enjoying a hot cup of coffee and one of his cigars. He had wondered at the time why he had not seen Frank and the boy at the services but had excused them because of the terrible storm. Then there was the pounding on the door and Frank was standing in the kitchen before the priest could get up from the table.

"It's Sonny, Father. Dr. Macek said that I should get you."

At first the priest had not fully comprehended.

"What's the trouble?" he asked, getting ready to pour a cup of coffee for Frank.

"The doc says that he has pneumonia bad." Frank's voice was anguished. "He may not live through the night."

Then the priest understood and the realization made him feel sick. Trying hard to be calm, fighting for control of his emotions, he said, "Get my car and meet me at the side door of the church."

As a priest, part of his sacred duties was giving the sacraments to the dying. During his many years in the parish he had baptized the newly born, blessed the newly wed, and had anointed the very sick and the dead many times. But never had he learned to perform any of those rites without becoming personally involved. Many times when he was with the very ill he felt himself a failure as a priest. So strongly was he affected by the loss of each soul that he could never find the right words of comfort for the family. Frequently he had rehearsed, while on his way to the sanctuary or en route to the sick call, platitudes of condolences to utter to those who were watching and waiting. But when the time came to use them, his mind was blank.

That night, as he hurried to the sanctuary to obtain the sacrament for Sonny, his mind kept saying, pleading, "Not the boy. Please, not our boy."

At the ambry when he removed the holy oils, he fully realized, perhaps for the first time, how strong his affections for the boy had grown. In the darkened church, he could hear the rain beating down on the slate roof and drumming against the large windows made almost invisible in the darkness. He asked himself if he had been wrong to become so attached to another human being. After all, he was a man who had given up the privileges of having a family, and what had he done? He had let a small boy burrow his way into his affection as if the boy were his own son. How many times had he, when Sonny was still a baby, found excuses to visit Frank so that he could hold the child in his arms? How many times, when the boy was toddling around Frank's shop, had he invented excuses to bring toys and gifts to Sonny? And then there were the outings that he had planned, like the one to Nelson Ledges. He had made them sound so casual, as if he had just been driving by and had thought that it would be wonderful to take the child for a drive in the country.

One time, he and Frank had quarreled over his attentions to the boy. Frank had accused him of trying to play the role of the godfather in fairy tales. Any of the boy's slightest wishes were granted as if the priest had only to wave a magic wand. Frank had insisted that the priest's lavish gifts were spoiling the boy, leading him to believe that he could have anything if he only wished for it. The priest had defended himself and his generosity, but in the end he had been forced to admit that what he had been doing was wrong for the boy. All of his gift giving had stopped except for special occasions like birthdays, Christmas, and Easter. And then his gifts were confined to utilitarian items rather than to his giving luxury things.

The priest steadied himself against the wall of the sanctuary that horrible night as he placed the holy oils into his carrying case along with his stole. He prayed for Sonny and for the strength to do what he had to do if Sonny were meant to be taken from him. And at that moment he resolved to confine his relationship with the boy to being no more than the parish priest.

Shaking off the unhappy memory, the priest replaced the photos and addressing himself to Mopsy, who was dozing next to his chair, said, "We pulled him through all right. We sat up all night with that boy while his fever raged on. Shortly after daybreak, he was out of danger."

Thinking about the happy ending, he sat down in his chair and, with his hand hanging over the arm of the chair, scratched Mopsy's ears.

"No one who had been there could have called that neglect, Mopsy. Frank and the doctor never left the boy's side. I'm sure that they talked him out of his fever. And me—I raced home and got a bag of coal out of the cellar and a can of coffee. All I did was to feed the fire and pour strong black coffee. The boy was magnificent. He fought like a Spartan."

The sound of her master's voice roused the dog, and she came around to the front of his chair and looked up at him with tongue out and ears cocked. Being alone as much as he was, the priest had formed the habit of speaking his thoughts out loud to the dog. And Mopsy, as if guided by some animal instincts which told her of her master's need, always sat and listened with rapt attention. There were times when she looked as if she were about to reply, and if she had, the priest probably would not have been too concerned about it.

"One thing about the boy," the priest continued, "one thing that no one can question is the boy's honesty. That says a lot for Frank. I've never known the boy to lie or to take anything that wasn't his. So what's all the fuss about? Let the courts and lawyers look into the boy's case. He's happy, healthy, and honest. What else could anyone demand?"

As if to answer his question, a new thought flashed through his mind like an exploding firecracker: education!

The priest had suddenly realized that he had never checked to see how the boy was doing in school. He had never discussed the boy's accomplishments with Frank since their quarrel over the gifts. He had never made school grades a topic of his chats with Sonny simply because he wished to keep their relationship strictly on a casual basis. He didn't want Sonny to get the idea that his interest went deeper than that of a friend of his uncle. And he had never talked to the sisters about the boy. To do so, he felt, might be dangerous. He was afraid that if the sisters discovered that he had a special interest in one of their pupils they might give the boy extra attention without their being aware of what they were doing. He, therefore, had no idea of what grades Sonny was receiving nor did he even know in which grade he was in. Perhaps he had assumed that the boy was quite bright and was, naturally, doing well. But what if he wasn't? What was his attendance like? What if the courts examined the boy's school records and discovered that the boy's education was being neglected? Perhaps he didn't know that the boy was a truant.

Monsignor Jindra decided to find out about that right away. He would chat with the principal of his school. He would have to be casual about it—unconcerned, but interested. He had been sitting in his home in his shirt sleeves, without his collar, since the doctor had left. He debated on how he should dress for his chat with Sister Anita and decided that the shirt sleeve approach would be the most casual. He would certainly want to convey to the nun that his visit was far from being a formal conversation between the parish's priest and the principal of the parish's school.

Having made up his mind as to the matter of dress and the tone of the conversation, he strolled out of his home and across the street to the sisters' home. He even took the willing Mopsy with him to add to the air of informality. Playing fully the role of a man walking his dog, he meandered into the yard of the convent, around the side of the building, and then on into its back yard. As he had expected, most of the sisters were outdoors. Usually in the summertime, the hours in the midafternoon were the sisters' time for recreation. As he turned into the back yard, he saw four of the sisters in a loud game of badminton. He thought that if they would put more muscle power and less lung power into their game, the results would be better. Mopsy, anticipating some fun, dashed into the game, increasing the laughter.

Several of the sisters were crocheting. Sister Anita was tatting lace around a doily, her gold-rimmed glasses perched on the end of her tiny nose. She was rather a large woman with a round, pink face.

As he was spied entering the yard, all activity stopped. The sisters who had been sitting rose to their feet. The badminton players abandoned the shuttlecock, upon which Mopsy pounced. The sisters, facing him, chorused, "Good afternoon, Monsignor."

Mopsy had brought the shuttlecock to him, and taking it

from her, he scolded her gently. Throwing the bird back into the game, he said in a manner reserved for the convent grounds, "Please, please, Sisters, don't let me interrupt. I would just like to pass the time of day with our Sister Anita."

The nun he had mentioned by name had been sitting under the grape arbor on an iron bench with Sister Cecilia, the school's music teacher. Quickly, quietly, she scurried away and sat on one of the lawn chairs among the crocheting group. Sister Anita and all the other nuns remained standing until he had seated himself on the bench. Then the badminton players started their game and included Mopsy in it.

"School will be starting soon," he said by way of opening the conversation. "I hope that everything is going well."

"Yes, Reverend Father. All is well."

"Do we have any last-minute needs that should be attended to?"

"I can't think of anything," the principal said.

"I have been going over our accounts," he fibbed, "and I find that I have a few extra dollars that could be put to good use."

"The Reverend Father is most considerate in providing for our school."

"I just want to be sure that we give our children every possible opportunity."

"The Reverend Father can be sure that we shall."

"Good! I'm sure of it. However, I was thinking about the classrooms in particular. Are they in good repair?"

"Yes, Father. Mr. Patek has sanded and varnished all the desks needing attention."

"The rooms themselves," he fenced, looking for some way to bring the talk to his main purpose, "how are they?"

"I'd say that they are in fairly good condition."

"Are any of them in serious need of painting? I'm sure that I could get Mr. Novak to splash on new paint where needed."

"The boys' lavatory has been somewhat abused."

"Does it need painting?" he asked as if he were seriously concerned.

"No, Reverend Father," she laughed, thinking that his concern was about the possibility of the walls being marked up. "I think that the plumbing needs looking after. Mr. Patek has complained about faucets that fail to turn off. Perhaps he could explain it better. He said that he would talk to you about it."

"I'll make it a point to see him," the priest brightened, feeling that now he had his opening. "I could get Mr. Novak to repair the valves and perhaps decrease our water bills."

Sister Anita fastened her attention on her lace to avoid looking at him and murmured, "He might check also the plumbing in the sisters' rest room in the school. Not everything works satisfactorily there."

"I'll do that by all means, Reverend Sister. I'm sure that Mr. Novak will be pleased to have the work, and I feel that he will do the job correctly."

"Thank you, Reverend Father," said the nun. "It would give us all great peace of mind if Mr. Novak were to check things carefully."

"By the way, Sister, how is his boy, Sonny, doing?"

"Anthony, Reverend Father?"

The priest recognized her question as being as much a reprimand as a correction. She had always maintained nothing less than a strict formality in her dealings with her pupils and their parents.

Taking advantage of her correction to mask his personal interest, he said, "Oh? Is that the boy's name?"

"Anthony's doing quite well, really."

"That's nice. I sometimes worry about those children who have no mothers to prod them through school. Sometimes men who try to be mothers fail in that task."

Perhaps Sister Anita was surprised by his statement, but she was nonetheless pleased by the observation. Apparently the remark was just what she needed to feel relaxed enough to break into a real conversation with her superior, for suddenly her whole manner and tone changed to one of great warmth.

"You know, Father, I have felt the same way. It was always my mother and not my father who heard our lessons. So naturally, I have been concerned about Anthony."

"And has your concern been justified?"

"His recitation of catechism is fairly good," she reported with great pleasure.

"Oh, I am delighted!" the priest exclaimed, mostly because he felt that he should make that kind of reply.

"But I think, Reverend Father, that his ability is more of a credit to his memory than to his education."

The priest sneaked a quick glance into the face of the nun and felt that he had detected more of a glint of admiration than of regret.

"And what of his other studies, Sister?"

"He reads very well and extensively. I think that that must be his uncle's influence. I understand that the two of them make frequent trips to the library, and that they spend many of their evenings together reading. Of course I'm not familiar with everything he reads, so I can't assume responsibility for his guidance there."

"Of course not," the priest said with a wave of his hand to show that he would not hold her responsible. "But it would seem that you have been concerned for your young charge."

"No more than any other student, really," she said, and the priest felt that she was speaking the truth. "If some aspects of his education have been of greater interest to me, it may be because of his mind which shows some signs now and then of a creative impulse."

"Oh? I'm not sure that I understand," he replied, trying hard to keep the conversation on an impersonal but educational level.

"Anthony seems to have the ability to see far beneath the surface of many things. He seems able to draw more out of his work than most children do. To penetrate deeper, so to speak."

"Is that bad?" he wondered.

"No, Reverend Father. But that characteristic needs to be directed properly. Like many creative people, he is capable of deep feelings about many things. The danger is that his deep feelings may cause him to react strongly. He could overturn the boat and drown himself."

The priest was amazed at the nun's insight and reprimanded himself for not being fully aware of it before.

"He's a very sensitive, creative boy who probably imagines himself to be bad luck to those people closest to him," she summed it up.

"Is there anything that we should be doing or something that we should not be doing?"

Sister Anita was quite pleased with the conversation. She had never thought that the parish priest was so interested in her pupils. She had always respected the time and effort that he contributed to the school as a whole. Now she was pleased that he was equally interested in individual students. Perhaps, she thought, they might get together and discuss other problems.

"I wish I knew," she said, wanting to follow through on this one topic first. "Maybe you could look into things. I feel that the boy is very fond of his uncle and would like to make some kind of compensation for what he believes the uncle has sacrificed."

"I'll make it a point to do just that, Sister. But are you saying that we have in the boy some good college material?"

She shook her head sadly. "I'm afraid that there may not be enough money to get him through high school, much less college."

"Let's assume that I could find a benefactor who would sponsor his college education. Would there be a chance?"

"Certainly he has the ability. But I'm afraid that he feels so indebted to his uncle that his thoughts are on earning a paycheck as soon as possible. That's one of the things I meant when I said that he could make a wrong decision."

"One of the things . . . ?"

"The others could be an act of violence or an outright criminal act. It all depends upon how desperate he feels."

"In which area of the curriculum is he the strongest?"

"His arithmetic is outstanding. If I were to suggest a career, I'd bet on engineering. That's probably his uncle's influence. I feel sure that the uncle has been instructing him in mathematics. I believe that the boy already knows a considerable amount about the applications of geometry and trigonometry without being fully aware of the absolute theories."

"Is that your personal conclusion, or is it based on evidence?"

"I'd say evidence. I have some of his worksheets. He solves problems in mathematics using principles far beyond those taught in the textbook. He'll be in the eighth grade next year, and I feel that he already uses techniques taught in algebra."

"Isn't that interesting?" the priest mused. "Then you are saying that if some benefactor were to look at his scholastic record, he would be impressed?"

"If you mean Anthony's school marks, I'd say yes."

"You have some reservations?"

"Only in his overwhelming desire to do something to reward or to repay his uncle and to do it quickly."

"How is his school attendance? Does he skip school?"

"Rarely does he miss a day. I would think that he enjoys school although, like most boys, he pretends to hate it."

The priest laughed at her insight and said sincerely, "I have always been impressed, Sister, by your personal interest in our children. Now I am delighted."

"Does the Reverend Father have a special interest in this boy?"

He paused, searching for a way of replying that would not involve his telling a falsehood.

"Let's say, Sister, that I'm interested in any pupil whose potential is such as to bring credit to our school and, of course, to our teachers."

"You are most kind, Reverend Father."

"Not at all," he replied, delighted with the nun's professional abilities. "I have been pleased by your devotion to the education of our parishioners. I want always to encourage your work. If it seems that I have been remiss, it's because we haven't communicated properly. I shall always make myself available for a conference with you, Sister."

Rising, the priest gave all of his teachers his brightest smile and followed it with his gayest wave. He felt quite pleased as he departed. It took only a snap from his fingers to induce Mopsy to stop her play and follow him.

Back in his own parlor, he told the dog, "We have nothing to worry about. No one can say that the boy's education is being neglected. Now there's only one area left. It's Frank himself. That's the criticism. It's the way Frank and the boy get on together that bothers people. I'll have to talk to him about cutting the boy loose, and I'll do it tonight. Right after dinner I'll see Frank and set him straight. He only needs a little jogging."

Feeling quite content, he took off his shoes and stretched his legs out. He felt so good that he thought he should apportion another cigar for himself. He usually limited himself to four cigars a day. One after mass, one after lunch, one after dinner, and his favorite one, the evening cigar he smoked while walking Mopsy. Today, he felt that he should have a special treat.

So in his shirt sleeves with his collar off, his shoes off, and with a cigar sending aromatic blue clouds of smoke drifting over his head, he relaxed. He looked at the radio across the room and thought of turning the ball game on. But he was too comfortable to get up. Even when there was a knock on his screen door, he felt too content with the world to move.

"Come on in!" he called, thinking that it was the paper boy or the woman who cooked his dinner.

If he was surprised to see Mr. Maresh the attorney walk in, he didn't show it. He might even have been delighted at the unexpected visit. Here was the enemy entering his own parlor, and he had enough ammunition to destroy his castle.

"Mr. Maresh!" he exclaimed. "This is an unexpected pleasure. Do come in, and please forgive my informal attire."

The priest neither rose to greet him nor made any attempt to put his shoes on.

"Pull up a chair," he said nonchalantly. "Help yourself to a cigar there on the smoking stand."

The attorney beamed, for he had not expected to find the priest in such a relaxed mood.

"I'm interrupting I know, Father. So please forgive me."

"Not at all. Not at all. My door is always open although I may not be prepared for visitors."

"Would you rather I came at another time?"

"Are you here on formal business?"

"Not really. I'd just like to chat for a while."

"Delighted!" said the priest. "Nothing could please me more. The fact is I was hoping someone would come by for a friendly chat. I've had a very busy day, and I would appreciate the relaxation of a friendly chat."

"Perhaps I should come back some other time. . . ."

"Oh! If you wish this to be a formal visit, I'll be happy to put on my shoes and even my collar. Trouble is that my feet get hot. Do your feet get hot, counselor?"

The attorney tried to laugh, but felt a little bit embarrassed. He didn't know whether to leave or to stay and the priest was enjoying the man's discomfort.

"I'm here on a parish matter, but the nature of it is such as to warrant informality," the attorney began.

"Wonderful! Do have a cigar. You don't smoke them? Well, if you'd rather have a cigarette, please enjoy yourself. We're two old friends. Let's not stand on ceremony."

"In this matter," the attorney began, "some of your parishioners have retained me to petition our courts to investigate the guardianship of a boy named Anthony Novak."

"Fine!" said the priest, unexpectedly. "I'm glad to see you donating your time so generously to such a worthy cause, and I'm sure that your motives have nothing at all to do with your political aspirations."

Again the attorney was surprised and again he showed it.

"We all want to do what is right," he said.

"Absolutely! Now, how can I contribute to your worthy task?"

"Well, Monsignor, I thought that first we should get a line on Frank Novak."

"You're right!"

"We should know where he came from and all about his past history."

"Good thinking!"

"I've tried to trace him down, but as you probably know, there are more Novaks in the directory than there are Smiths."

"True. Very true, counselor."

"I've traced a Frank Novak who used to live in Maple Heights. He had a wife who ran off with a man who owned a feed store. Now this could be the same Frank Novak. That's where you can help, Monsignor."

"Tell me how. Tell me how."

"Perhaps you could tell me about our Frank Novak. He must have transferred here from another parish. A: Where did he come from? B: What were the circumstances of his leaving? C: What about his so-called relatives in Kansas? I haven't been able to locate anyone there who was aware of a Novak in Cleveland."

"Those are all very good questions," the priest said honestly.

"Thank you, Monsignor."

"If you knew all of those answers, you would certainly know all about Frank."

"Precisely," the attorney beamed. "That's why I need

your help. I figure that you are the only person who can fill in the blanks for us."

"Perhaps."

The attorney flipped open a notebook and held a pencil over it expectantly, saying, "Let's start with A."

"There's nothing that I would care to tell you about Frank Novak."

"Come now, Father. This is serious business. I could have you subpoenaed."

"I consider all of my information as being privileged."

"Certainly, Monsignor, much is a matter of record."

"Church records, counselor. Do you think that I would let my parish records be used as testimony, perhaps, against one of my parishioners? Absolutely not!"

"The courts might find you in contempt."

"That's quite possible," replied the priest. "But I would rather be found in contempt by an earthly court than found negligent when I am judged in the court having complete jurisdiction over me."

"But, Monsignor," the attorney persisted, "for all we know, Frank may have been in prison. He may be a murderer."

"You are quite correct, Mr. Maresh. Frank could be all those things and worse. But his past is no concern of mine. My duties are to forgive him his trespasses, not to discuss them."

"Are you saying that you will not co-operate with the courts?"

"Not at all, counselor. I would be quite pleased to tell the court how well the boy is doing in my school. I'd be pleased to tell anyone of his academic achievements. I would like to tell the court how highly he is regarded by the boys his own age. I hear that they have a lot of respect for his ability to play baseball. Consider the activities he's engaged in! I think that his activities are enough to indicate robust health. So we have here a boy who is strong and healthy both morally and physically, and you want to dig into a past for some kind of evidence? You know that even a criminal's past cannot be a part of the evidence in a trial. So what are you trying to do?"

"I only want to help the boy," Mr. Maresh said as an excuse.

"If that's true, and I have no reason to doubt you, then look at the boy as he is today."

"We must consider the boy as for tomorrow also," the attorney responded wisely.

"Absolutely! Those are my thoughts exactly."

"And we should protect our parish from scandal."

"My concern," replied the priest, "is to protect our parish from scandal mongers. The Bible has something to say about that."

The attorney folded his blank notebook and stuffed it back into his brief case.

"I'm sorry," he said coldly, "to have bothered the monsignor."

"No bother at all," pleaded the priest. "I'm here only to serve my people."

Mr. Maresh laughed wryly. "I certainly didn't get anything out of this visit."

"Come around with something concrete. Show me some evidence of a crime that Sonny or Frank has committed. Show me some evidence of real neglect, and I will help you. But be sure that you're talking about today."

"I might say that your opinion is biased, Monsignor."

"That would be a mistake. I might say from the pulpit that Mr. Maresh tried to use the publicity from the plight of a poor orphan to advance his own political aspirations."

"That conclusion would be unfounded," was the hasty reply of the attorney.

"No less than yours is."

Shyly and embarrassed, the attorney got to his feet. "I'm glad that you chose the church instead of the law. I would hate to have you as an opponent."

"Mr. Maresh, please don't be distressed by our conversation. My antagonism is for the cause you support, and not for you."

With that, the priest arose and extended his hand, saying, "May God go with you always, Mr. Maresh."

As the footsteps of the attorney were heard pounding down the porch steps, the priest ruffled the fur around Mopsy's neck and said, "There are times—a few times—when I like my work very much."

7

For the priest, the rest of the afternoon seemed to be dragging. He kept watching the clock, wondering if Frank and the boy had returned yet. Their evening meal, the priest knew, would be eaten at about five o'clock. Certainly on a day that they had spent fishing, they would eat no later than five. If their fishing luck were good, Frank would fry the whole catch right away. They would eat a hot meal and snack on cold fish the rest of the evening. The matter of the evening meal was important because he did not want Sonny present during his talk with Frank. Usually after the evening meal, the boy fled the home for Dusek's vacant lot and a ball game. Or the boy would join the gang on Cerny's front steps and talk the evening away. The most important thing was that Sonny had to be out of the house.

The priest padded in his sock feet over to the buffet in the dining room. In the top drawer, under the napkins was a velvet-lined, silver jewelry box that had been his mother's. The box was very old. It had been on his mother's dresser as long as he could remember. In it his mother had kept her few precious ornaments: a cameo brooch, a lavaliere with a tiny diamond in it, a gold locket, and a string of garnet beads. The box was badly tarnished. The silver had blackened and on the lid there was a large patch where the silver had changed to a bright, iridescent purple. When he picked the box up, he felt the gumminess of its surface which he didn't like and made a mental note for the hundredth time to ask the woman who cleaned his house periodically to include the box when she polished the silverware.

Inside the box was a number of bills. This was the money he received for wedding ceremonies. To himself he called the box and its contents his "happiness collection." The use of the money was strictly relegated for happy uses. He bought his cigars with that money or used it to send gifts to his friends and relatives. Removing all of the bills, he counted forty-two dollars. Pocketing the money, he left the box on top of the buffet and closed the drawer. He was determined to give the money to Frank to spend on the boy. How he would accomplish this, he did not know. So he returned to his chair to think of some scheme which Frank might find face saving enough for taking the money.

His first thought was to offer the money as a loan, but he immediately knew that Frank would see through that disguise. Frank would not accept a loan which would be impossible to pay back. His next idea was to give Frank the money as an advance payment for the work he would do on the school's plumbing. But this brought up another problem. Frank charged fifty cents an hour for his labor. To earn forty dollars meant that he would have to work two full weeks to earn that amount. The work in the school would hardly take two days. Frank would not stand for being overpaid. Only one alternative remained: the priest would have to present the money as a gift and get Frank to accept it for what it was. But how?

Father Jindra knew that there was no possible way he could cajole Frank into taking the money. The best way to proceed would be to lay all the facts on the line. He would tell Frank of the day's events. He might run the risk of Frank's breaking Attorney Maresh's jaw, but that too would have to be handled. Perhaps Dr. Macek would set the jaw at a discount.

"Now listen to reason, Frank," the priest rehearsed a possible dialogue in his mind. "You've got to take this money and get some decent clothes for that boy. We've (he would deliberately use *we* to let Frank know that as godfather he had some rights and obligations too) simply got to send that boy to school decently dressed. So take the money. It's not for you; it's for the boy. Spend it all on the boy if it will suit your conscience, but get him dressed! Buy underwear and socks by the dozens. Shirts he needs badly. And for heaven's sake, get him a good raincoat!"

Frank would surely protest. Frank would argue that the boy was strictly his responsibility and that he could manage.

"I'm not questioning your ability or the sincerity of your industry," he would reply. "You're down on your luck. We've got to think of the boy. If it suits you better, don't spend the money all at once. Get a little each week. It's all right to let the boy think that the money's coming from your work. I don't care how you do it just so long as the boy looks good."

Again Frank would protest, and the priest would have to tell him, "Some of your neighbors want the courts to look into your guardianship of the boy. They feel that the boy is being neglected. And you know that we can't have anyone nosing around the circumstances under which you gained custody of the boy. He has not been legally adopted. It was I who granted you the care of the child, and I warned you at the time that I could revoke that right. That was our bargain."

The last statement, the priest felt sure, would both win

and end the argument. The next point he would have to make would be the one on their relationship.

"Frank," he would say, "don't you think that it's about time you cut Sonny loose and let him take care of himself? Don't you think that you should stop dragging him along on all of your hikes? Shouldn't the boy be left more to his own devices?"

Frank would certainly not accept that attack too easily. Those could very well be fighting words. He would have to add quickly and diplomatically, "I'm not implying what you're doing is wrong; I'm just saying that it looks bad. Tongues are wagging."

Being satisfied with both his own line of reasoning and the rehearsal, the priest settled back into his chair. Mopsy, who had disappeared without his being aware of it, came trotting to his chair with the evening paper in her mouth. That meant that the woman who did his cooking had arrived and was in the kitchen. Taking the paper, he patted the dog, saying out loud to her, "If there was another orphaned boy in the neighborhood, I'd turn him over to Frank too."

In order to kill time, he tried hard to read the paper, but, by the time he got to the sports page, he couldn't remember anything he had read. Concentrating hard, he put into his mind that the Cleveland Indians were getting good pitching but their hitting had slumped and their bench was weak.

"When I talk to Frank," he told himself, "I'll just have to tell him that he's been too weak with the boy. No! It only *looks* like he's been too weak."

"Frank weak?" another section of his mind responded. "That man's got a will that's like his anvil. It's undentable. Didn't he raise that boy against all odds?"

"Then what is the complaint?" a third member of the gallery in his mind demanded.

The priest shrugged off all of his thoughts and returned to his newspaper.

By the time the cook had called him to dinner, he had decided that he'd talk to Frank honestly and explain the whole situation to him. Frank was a reasonable man, and he would understand. As for the meal he ate, he hardly tasted it and probably didn't remember what he had eaten. He refused the dessert and gulped his coffee. He had made up his mind now and was in a hurry to say to Frank what he thought had to be said before he forgot the precise wording. If, when he got there, Sonny was still in the house, he'd send the boy out to Krejci's candy store for some cigars and an ice cream bar for himself.

Quickly, the priest slipped into his shoes, donned his backward collar, adjusted his maroon cloth, and even though it was a very warm evening, he shrugged into his black coat. On top of his thinning gray hair, he set his Panama hat. Followed by Mopsy, he went out the back door and pulled himself into his Model A. Mopsy scooted past him and took up her co-pilot's position on the front seat.

After backing the car successfully out of his driveway, the priest aimed it rather than drove it to the fixit shop. He had never been particularly fond of cars. A car was one of those necessities that went with his duties. When he first came to the parish as its new pastor, he had a horse and carriage. After fourteen years with a horse as a partner in sick calls, he was forced to retire the aging animal. He bought his first car then. He immediately discovered that the horseless carriage lacked much of the common sense that horses had. For instance, the car could not take him home after a long night of vigil with a dying man. Control of the horse required the use of his hands only and those only when the traffic was heavy. The car always required the co-ordination of his two feet with his two hands. If he had really accepted the motor car, it was with the understanding that driving the car was one of the sacrifices he had to make to progress.

At the fixit shop, he stopped the Model A and set the brake. As a parking job, it might not have been too good, but he was satisfied to have stopped in the general area of the curb near to where he was going. With the dog in the lead, he went through the front door of the shop. Mopsy made a wild dash to the kitchen in response to something that her senses had communicated. When the priest arrived, he found the boy and the dog on the floor, rolling about in a heated wrestling match.

"Hi, Sonny. Where's Unk?"

"Hi, Father. Pasek's meat grinder broke. He's there trying to fix it."

The priest sat down in the wooden rocker Frank had made. The room showed its usual cleanliness. Two beds, really cots, were against the walls, that is, one was against the outside wall and the other was against the partition to the shop. They were head to head, with a large square table holding a lamp occupying the corner. In the center of the kitchen end of the room was a table, also made by Frank, unpainted but bleached white from frequent scrubbings. In the quiet air of the room, the priest could smell the lingering odor of fried fish.

"Were the Little People good to you today?" he asked conversationally.

"Oh, boy! Yes."

Sonny picked himself up from the floor and slid onto a footstool. The dog worried at his unbuttoned shirt cuff.

"Unk caught five bullheads. Three were of a nice size.

The other two were youngsters, so he threw them back. You know Unk."

The priest nodded. That was Frank. He took from the lakes and the wild orchards only what he could eat. He was a conserver rather than a destroyer.

"We got there early and found some nice mushrooms," the boy went on.

Again the priest nodded. There was still in the air the slight odor of mushrooms fried in butter. He wondered if he should not have come earlier and had supper with them.

"What time did you go out?" the priest asked, sincerely interested.

"About five, I think. It takes almost two hours to walk there. And Unk likes to do his walking in the morning whenever possible."

"That's rough on you, isn't it?"

"How so, Father?"

"Getting up so early in the morning and taking a hike like that."

"I don't mind it."

"Wouldn't you rather be doing something else?"

"Like what, Father?"

"Oh, I don't know," the priest shrugged, feeling a bit sorry that he had brought up the topic. It seemed to him that the boy had picked up from his uncle the habit of insisting on being specific. "Whatever boys your age like to do best. Like maybe staying in bed and sleeping late."

"Oh no, Father. I like to go out with Unk. We have a lot of fun together. And early in the morning is the best time to hike. The air is cool and smells nice and fresh."

"You really like it?"

"Sure! But I worry about Unk. At first I couldn't keep

up with him," laughed the boy. "And now he can't keep up with me. But please don't tell him I said so."

"You may have to give up some of these hikes soon, you know."

"Why?"

"Your uncle is growing older as you already know, and so are you. Soon you'll have other interests to follow. In a few years you'll be going to high school, and you'll find yourself in a lot of school activities, baseball, football, basket ball, and maybe even track. There'll be clubs you'll want to join. High school will be a whole new world."

"As long as Unk wants to go and wants me to go with him, I'll be shagging his footsteps. He's more fun than all those things you said. I'll never let him go alone!"

"You'll never let him go alone?" the priest repeated in his astonishment.

"Did he let me go it alone? He was everything I had. Maybe one day I will be everything he has."

The priest nodded and looked for another topic. In the dialogues he had rehearsed earlier, he had not anticipated the feelings of Sonny.

"I'm glad you had a good day," he said. "Do you think Unk will be back soon?"

"I think so, Father. If it's something simple, he'll fix it there. But if it's something bad, he'll have to fix it here. He'll be back soon. This is library night."

The priest had noticed the books piled on the table. He would have liked to have examined them, but he intended to keep his pledge to himself not to invade their privacy. He would not let himself be more than a friend of the family. The boy must not see him as being more than the uncle's very good friend. Such was the pledge he had made a little over two years ago.

The boy smiled brightly at his uncle's very good friend

and asked, "Would you want to see what else the Little People left for me?"

If the priest was hesitant, it was because he was not altogether unfamiliar with the ways of small boys. A frog or a toad could very well jump out of the box the boy was taking down from the shelf over his bed. Maybe there would be a turtle or a snake inside. He scanned the boy's face for a possible clue, but he saw only sparkling eyes and a pleasant smile. Carefully and amusedly, he lifted the cover. The sight of the money was a surprise greater than he could have expected.

Puzzlement being his first reaction, the priest said, "Where, or how did you get it?"

"It was in the elderberry bushes at the park." There was an unmistaken hint of triumph in the boy's voice.

"Now that you have it, what will you do with it?" asked the priest, wondering if the boy knew the proper steps to take following such a find.

The boy returned to his stool. Mopsy climbed back into his lap and stretched herself across the boy's knees. Sonny scratched behind her ears.

"First I'm going to get Unk down to Dr. Mikesh. His eyes are so bad that he can't do much reading any more. And you know how much he likes to read."

The priest began to say something about found money, but checked himself with the determination not to intervene.

"Is that so?" he intoned. "I hadn't noticed."

"It's only bad with close work. Sometimes I'm afraid that he may injure himself in the shop doing close work."

"What will you do with the rest of the money?" He decided that he would use the money as a way of exploring the boy's mind. Now he might find out what the boy was really like. The money could tell him. He realized that he could be sorry that he uncovered something that would be better for him not to see, but he had to risk it.

"Then I'm going to buy Unk a fine overcoat like the one in Slivka's window. He only has that old leather jacket. He should have an overcoat, don't you think? For church at least."

"That's another ten dollars," said the priest. "What are your plans for the rest? Will you buy a shopful of bubble gum?"

The priest smiled at the boy encouragingly. He had worked him into a trap. Now he would have the best weapon to use against Frank.

"I'm going to . . . I would like to . . . I think I will . . . I'm going to buy Unk . . . a . . . Ford . . . car!"

"What?" the priest exclaimed. The answer was not what he had expected. "A Ford car? What for?"

"You know how Unk likes to fish and go looking for mushrooms and berries and apples and black walnuts and things?"

"Yes, of course. He's always done that for as long as I've known him, and I've known him for about twenty-five years."

"Then you know that when he goes out into the country, he takes the Broadway streetcar and rides it to the end of the line. Then he walks way out Miles Avenue past Warrensville. He hunts his mushrooms or whatever he's after, walks back to the streetcar line, and comes back home. Sometimes he catches the four o'clock car to get out there before the sun kills the mushrooms."

"So?"

"So he spends more time coming and going than he does out in the fields. If he had a car, he wouldn't have to walk so much. And he could go farther out too."

To the priest's mind came the image of Frank's brass-hooded Chevrolet and how Frank disappeared every Sunday after the first mass. The car had been the first luxury Frank had sold when he had set up his shop.

"Unk could go to many different places too. Maybe he could even go way out on the West Side," the boy went on. "Or maybe he could go out to one of those lakes that Pasek goes to and catch some bass or trout maybe. But he'd need glasses before he could drive, I think."

Leaning his head against the back of the rocker, the priest closed his eyes. How amazing was the boy's insight! How much the boy had known or been aware of that he, supposedly Frank's best friend, had not seen. But he mustn't let the boy sidetrack the main issue. He would have to lead the conversation back to the moral issue.

Sonny continued his list with, "I will get him one of those gas heaters for his workshop. Then we can make the coal shed into a garage for his Ford. He'll like that."

The thought went through the priest's mind that if Sonny had only said something about spending the money on himself, things would be much easier. But to the boy, he said, "Can you really spend the money? Is it really yours?"

"The Little People left it for me. For me or for anyone else who happened along."

"I think that there's a difference between the money and a bunch of mushrooms."

"How?" the boy was inquisitive, not belligerent.

"The fish in the lake and the apples that grow in the wild fields were put there by God. They are for man to use. Money is a thing made by man and must, therefore, belong to *a* man. Money is a man's property and regardless of the circumstances, it remains his property."

"It was abandoned," Sonny replied. "Like the coal along the railroad tracks. The box must have been there for weeks. See how wet it got? The tape along the sides has come unstuck. A caterpillar spun a cocoon between the lid and one side."

"Perhaps some robber hid it there."

"Finders keepers; losers weepers."

"How much is in the box?"

"One hundred tens and one hundred fives."

"Fifteen hundred dollars. That's a lot of money to abandon."

"I haven't heard of anyone losing that amount of money. And I haven't heard of a robbery like that, have you, Father?"

"No, I haven't read of anything like that in the papers."

"When Unk gets his car, he'll be able to go all over the city to fix things. He could have a telephone put in. A telephone would get him a lot more work. Then on Wednesdays he can have his day off anyplace. He's got to get a car!"

"And what about you? Is there nothing that you would want?"

"Like what?"

"Clothes? A bike maybe?"

"Not really. The car and the glasses and the coat come first. After that, things will be easier. Unk will have more jobs, and more money will be coming in for some of the things I need. You see, Father, Unk wants to be the one who brings in the bacon. This money is practically the only way I can help him."

The priest thought of the forty-two dollars in his pocket. He too had realized that only a large sum of money in one lump could help Frank.

"Will Unk take your money? You know him better than I do, but he doesn't seem like the kind of man who accepts such generous gifts so easily."

The priest's question had a double meaning. He wanted

to get some idea of Frank's stand on the "abandoned" money without the boy knowing it.

"Oh, yes. Whenever we go out scrounging together we always divvy up the findings. It was Unk who made the rule. I found it, so I can divvy it my way."

Before the priest could think of an answer, the boy asked, "Will you help me, Father?"

"Help you? How?"

"Unk might be a problem. He might not want to play the game now that I have something to share. Help me get him to an eye doctor. Help me get him some decent clothes. And help me with the car idea."

"I'll help you all I can," the priest assured him. He was about to add another statement with the word *right* in it, but thought it best to leave the matter where it was.

Getting to his feet, the priest said, "Tell Unk that I'll stop by later."

The dog, still in the boy's lap, watched his master go, expecting to be called. When she received no such command and after the front door had closed, she put her nose back into her paws and suffered the boy's face in her neck.

"Maybe on Sundays, when Unk goes out for a ride, he'll take me and let me take you. Would you like that Mopsy?"

8

"Sonny!"

The name was bellowed outside the back window.

"Come on in, Carl!" Sonny responded, and he hurried to get the shoe box back on the shelf over his bed. Mopsy had dashed to the back door, eager to greet the newcomer.

Carl Cerny was Sonny's very best friend. He lived across the street from Sonny and was such a constant visitor that Frank considered him a part of the family. Carl was the oldest of four children, and Frank had recognized the boy's need to find a "hangout" away from the babies. The fact that all the other children in Carl's family were girls made a daytime home for him a necessity. Sonny and Carl had quickly established a brotherly relationship.

"I thought the monsignor would never leave," said Carl. "I was scared I'd have to go in before I could see you."

Carl had dropped himself into the rocker. He held a playground-size baseball which he was sewing up with a curved upholsterer's needle. The ball was fourteen inches in circumference and was called an "indoor" ball for some reason which the boys never understood. It was a ball commonly used on playgrounds. The use of the ball did not endanger the other children who might be playing nearby. In fact, the game itself was called "softball." The size of the ball and its relative softness held many advantages over "hardball" requirements. The game could be played in a smaller area while adhering to most of the rules of the regular game. A minimum of equipment was required for the enjoyment of the game, namely a ball and a bat. In games of swift pitching, the catcher generally wore a fielder's glove. Sonny was his team's catcher but neither he nor anyone on the team owned a glove.

"So what's so important?" Sonny asked.

"We've got a game tomorrow," Carl announced. He was the team's pitcher and also assumed the role of the team's captain. As the team's manager, he roamed the area challenging and accepting challenges from other teams.

"Can you make it?" Carl asked, almost sure of the answer.

"Sure. What time?"

"Two in the afternoon."

"Easy. Who we playing?"

"Lourdes."

"Where?"

"There. We'll beat them this time, I bet."

"Sure," Sonny agreed. "Like they're nothing."

Carl went on sewing the ball, putting in first the stitches going diagonally from right to left. Later he would sew in those stitches which crossed the first set, ending with a neat pattern of x's.

"I was looking for you today," said Carl. "I thought I could get in a few warm-up pitches."

"I went fishing with Unk."

"Get anything?"

"That lousy, stinking lake hasn't got anything in it worth catching. Carp and bullheads! But Unk likes to fish and there's no place else to go without a car."

"I need to practice my fast ball and drop," Carl commented.

"Wish we had a car," Sonny moaned.

"Wish I could get my fast ball under control. Have you noticed? It takes off kind of like it's sailing."

"Lousy, stinking baseballs! That's what it is. They've been pounded flat. If we had a new ball to play with, it wouldn't sail."

"Fat chance! Where could we get one?"

"From the same place we'd get the car. Maybe the Ford guy would throw in a new baseball."

Both boys laughed at the joke.

"I wish I had a glove," Sonny said hopefully. "I'm the only guy who catches without a glove."

"That's okay," Carl reassured him. "I always tell the other guys that you're so tough you won't use a glove. They all think that you like to catch barehanded."

"Great stuff! So every guy comes in at me from third base like the Twentieth Century Limited to knock the toughness out of me."

"Quit complaining. You always stop them. Like a Bill Dickey you guard the plate."

"That's another thing: how come when you get us games to play we always play bigger guys? Next we'll be playing the Indians."

"We're too good is all. We're too good for our class. No one our size wants to play us."

"For once I'd like to get in a pushover game."

"Look at the experience we're getting," argued the captain-manager. "One day, Sonny, you and I are going to break into the big leagues. You catching and me pitching. You've got good hands, Sonny."

Turning his hands palms upward, Sonny examined them. They were about as wide across as they were from the heel of the palm to the fingers. The fingers were both thick and long. Several times his uncle had told him that he had the hands of a blacksmith. Just when it was that he was able to swing a twelve-pound maul, Sonny couldn't remember. The hammers in his uncle's shop had always fascinated him and had become his favorite toys. When other boys his age were pounding away with toy mallets, Sonny was hefting the ball peens and the sledges. Last year when he had gotten into a fight with a classmate— when one of the other boys had made some unkind remarks about his uncle's hikes—Sister Anita had lectured him soundly. Sonny had sailed into his antagonist and had inflicted serious damage to the boy's mouth.

Sister Anita had said, "You must never strike anyone in anger again! Promise me that. Your hands are like steel. I'm surprised at you. It's not like you to get angry. So promise me that next time you will keep your hands in your back pockets and count up to a hundred before you strike someone, and I won't mention this incident to your uncle." Sonny had promised and had kept his promise.

Carl had finished sewing the ball. He knotted the string and flipped the ball to Sonny. The catcher snatched it out of the air with one hand. Locking his fingers together, he mashed it into a flat, disclike sphere.

"Don't!" Carl complained. "Look what you've done. You've made it into an Easter egg."

Sonny laughed and tossed the ball into the air. Mopsy suddenly came to life and pranced around Sonny's chair, begging for a game.

"Don't let her get it," Carl advised. "It's the only ball the team has."

"Some team," Sonny snapped. "Can't even raise a buck to buy a ball."

"At least we've got a ball."

"It's more like a pillow."

"It's better than nothing."

"We've got two bats, and one of them is split. It's held together with nails and tape. The only good bat we have is the one Unk made on his lathe."

Seriously, not bragging, Carl said, "We can still beat Lourdes."

"So we beat Lourdes? So what?"

"So maybe next year we can get a backer and play Class E hardball, that's what. This softball is kids' stuff. We need to play league ball if we're ever going to get anywhere."

"Hardball means gloves for everyone and bats and balls and a mask and chest protector for the catcher. Where are we going to get equipment like that?"

"I'm thinking that maybe Mr. Nusek the undertaker will back us. Or maybe the monsignor will back us as a church team."

"Daydreams. If wishes were horses, beggars would ride."

"There's a chance."

"Nuts!"

"There is too! You and I are the best battery mates in this part of the city. I can pitch all day, and you know it."

"You'll need seven other guys unless you can strike out twenty-seven guys in every game."

Carl chuckled, "You catch me, and I'll strike them out."

"You're dreaming!"

"Maybe, but you're a good catcher, Sonny. You can make big league. You're a natural. You've got good hands. You've got a good throw to second base. And you've got guts."

"That's because I'm an idiot for letting you make a back-stop out of me."

Yes, Carl would have to agree, it was he who had made Sonny into a catcher. Carl had always wanted to be a pitcher, and a pitcher cannot practice without a target to throw at. Sonny had become that target years ago. On the sidewalk going to the back of the shop, Carl warmed up every day from the first spring thaw until the first snowfall. A chalked-in home plate had become a permanent feature on the flagstone. At first Sonny had been more interested in the exercise than in the sport. Whenever Carl came into the yard with a ball and suggested "throwing a few," Sonny had been agreeable. Had Sonny protested several times or if he had complained too much, Carl would have been forced to find someone else to receive his throws.

But that wasn't the whole of it. It took but a few games for Carl and the rest of the gang to see in Sonny the makings of a ball player. Sonny could hit. There was timing and power in his swing of the bat. Sonny was always relaxed, loose. Behind the plate he was a chatterbox full of confidence. With a bat gripped in his hands, he got the hits that won ball games. The one thing that always bothered Carl was that Sonny never seemed to care. He had the natural talent and didn't seem interested.

"You'll bat clean-up again tomorrow," Carl said. "You're the best stick man we have."

"With a clumsy bat that Unk made for me."

"It's a good bat. Unk put a lot of hits into it for you."

"I wouldn't know. I've never swung a real bat."

Suddenly Carl demanded, "What's the matter with you today?"

"What?"

"You. What's eating you?"

"Why?"

"You're nasty."

"Am I?"

"Yes. What's biting you?"

"Nothing."

"Something's eating at you."

"Maybe," Sonny shrugged.

"What?"

"I don't know. Maybe it's because we don't have anything."

"What do you want? Peanuts on an ice cream sundae?"

"I'd settle for the sundae," Sonny replied without smiling.

"Something's wrong with you."

"What?"

"Wish I knew."

"It's nothing that a couple of dollars wouldn't fix."

"Forget it!"

"Forget what?"

"Money is what you've got to forget," said Carl. "We ain't got none and we ain't going to get any."

"What if we can get some?"

"How? Rob a bank?"

"No. Maybe we can pick up a couple of bucks. Maybe a fiver."

"Fat chance!"

"Maybe."

"How?"

"Just maybe."

"And just maybe a scout for the Cleveland Indians will see me pitch and maybe they'll send me to one of their farm clubs and just maybe Mel Harder will show me the tricks of the trade and maybe I'll be the youngest pitcher to make the majors. Just maybe."

"How much is a bat?" Sonny interrupted suddenly.

"About a buck and a quarter at Jelinek's hardware store. Could be less at Sears."

"A glove?"

"No more than a couple of bucks."

"A ball?"

"Seventy-five cents. Maybe ninety."

"Five bucks ought to do it. Five bucks is all we need

and we can go out tomorrow looking like a ball team, right?"

"Okay, but where are you going to get five bucks from?"

"I'll have to think about it."

"While you're at it, think up a couple of bucks for me."

"Why?"

"If it's all that easy, you might just as well make it seven as five bucks."

"Don't be greedy," Sonny laughed. "If I should ask the Little People for too much, they may not give me any."

Carl nodded, rocking back and forth with each head movement.

"Your uncle's story. Don't tell me that you really believe in the Little People?"

"Sometimes you have luck that can't be explained in any other way. Spooky luck is what the Little People mean."

"If you can get five bucks, you can get seven. Then the two of us can go to Euclid Beach Park. We'd have ourselves a real day. Me? I'd stay on the roller coaster until I spent the whole buck."

"I've never been there," said Sonny. "What's it like?"

"The park or the roller coaster?"

"Both."

"There's all kinds of rides. Merry-go-round, derby race, crack-the-whip, dodge-ems, roller coaster, and a fun house and lots more. You'd have to see it for yourself."

"Maybe if Unk had a car we could go out there."

"Easy. And they say there's good fishing. Nice clean beaches. The place is a darb!"

"I'll bet."

Sonny wrestled with the idea of telling his very best friend about the shoe box he had found in the elderberries. He was sure that Carl's eyes would bug out. But he restrained himself for a reason he couldn't pin down. Maybe he doubted Carl's ability to keep a secret. Or maybe the money was too personal, a matter strictly between himself and his uncle. He wasn't quite sure why, but he felt that his secret must be kept awhile longer.

"How about a game of rummy?" Sonny suggested as a means of getting his mind off the shoe box.

"Naw. I've got to be going. Mom will be putting the babies to bed, and I've got some of my chores to do."

Having risen to go, Carl stood by the screen door and said, "The team is meeting in Dusek's field at about one to pepper the ball around and get in some practice. I'll see you then."

"Pillow practice," Sonny laughed. "Peppering a beanbag around!"

"Whatever's eating you, I hope it's had its gut full by tomorrow. I'd like to win that game."

"Sure we will," Sonny promised.

"Okay. Forget about the lousy luck you had fishing today and think about blasting out some homers tomorrow."

"Okay. S'long."

"S'long."

After the door had banged behind Carl and his footsteps indicated that he had left the yard, Sonny went over to his corner, took down the shoe box, and sat on the bed with the box in his lap. Mopsy jumped up and lay down beside him.

"Tomorrow morning," he told Mopsy, "I'll take five dollars and go down to Sears. I'll get a bat and a ball and a glove. Won't the kids' eyes pop when Sonny comes around for practice and throws in a new ball! I'll have my own bat, a real Louisville Slugger. I'll burn my initials into my bat right above the trade mark and on the strap of

my glove. The ball I'll give to the team. Won't that be
something? Sonny Novak with a bat and glove of his own!"

Sonny wondered how he might explain his sudden
wealth to his friends. A new bat, ball, and glove repre-
sented a fortune indeed. What would he tell them? Could
he say that he had earned it running errands for Pasek?
Such an explanation, he knew, was illogical. Everything
that he had earned in the past had gone into clothes and
schoolbooks with a dime here and there for a movie.

Would they believe that he had earned it peddling hand-
bills for Jelinek's hardware store? Unlikely. Most boys in
the neighborhood had done just that, and they all knew
what the pay was. He decided that he'd just tell them
that the Little People gave the money to him, and let
them figure it out for themselves. He enjoyed the thought
so much that he had to laugh at the reaction he imagined.
They all had heard Unk's tales about the Little People, so
why not give them the credit for his good fortune.

What about Unk? Could he really take five dollars out of
the box?

Sonny came to the conclusion that in all good faith he
could not pinch five dollars out of their money without
the consent of his uncle. But he felt sure that his uncle
would want him to have a glove and bat.

The slamming of the front door told him that his uncle
had returned. Sonny went into the shop followed by
Mopsy.

"The monsignor was here looking for you."

"Did he say what he wanted?" the uncle asked, seeming
to be hardly concerned at all. His attention was on a shaft
and a gear he had in his hand along with a tiny piece of
metal. He put micrometers to the small piece, read the
figures with a hand magnifying glass, and muttered, "Three
eighths of an inch square."

"The monsignor didn't say. I guess he only wanted to chat."

Unk dug into the cubbyholes where he stored his collection of scrap metal. The closest size he could find was a small bar of steel one-half inch square. Taking it to his bench, he locked it in a vise and began sawing off a piece seven eighths of an inch long.

"The key in the shaft broke off," he said to the boy. "Sloppy workmanship. The key was too small. Whoever put it together should have known it wouldn't last."

"You'll fix it and it will last forever."

"Sure," the uncle grinned. "Do it right, and you'll avoid trouble."

The boy held the broken piece in his hand.

"That didn't need to happen," the uncle went on. "A man must not think much of himself if he can't take pride in his work. How much more time would it have taken to do it right?"

"What does it matter?" asked the boy. "Who knows? You could fix it so that it would work. Who would know how good it was fixed or how bad?"

"Me," said the uncle. "I'd know. And I wouldn't like myself."

The boy left the shop to go to the back of the building. He returned with an armload of library books. The old man was still talking, perhaps to himself or perhaps to the boy.

"Do the thing right," he was saying. "It may seem harder, but it's a whole lot easier."

"That's what Holomecz should have done," the boy said quietly.

"What? What's that you're mumbling?" the uncle asked, squinting over the end of his nose at the small bit of metal.

"You know good and well what I'm saying. I'm talking about Holomecz. He only saw the horse—the easy way out. He didn't look to the consequences."

"You're talking gibberish."

"I'll tell you about it sometime," the boy replied. "Right now I've got to go out and return those library books you never read."

"I did too read them."

"Your eyes are so bad that you can only read the chapter headings."

"I haven't finished them all," the uncle complained.

"Shall I renew them for you?"

"No, when I want them again, I'll draw them out."

"I'll take Mopsy with me."

"Can you?"

"She'll stay outside and wait. I'll be right back, Unk."

"Won't you have to be in a hurry? The library stays open only until nine."

"That time bomb in the bedroom which you call a clock says that it's only a little after eight."

"Oh."

"Careful now. Don't cut your thumb off."

"Beat it, bum. Hit the road!"

"Poor Holomecz! In his studies you think he would have found out that no one would believe a beggar on horseback."

"Make sense, boy!"

"I'll tell you about it when I get back."

"In that case," replied the uncle, "please don't hurry."

9

When the priest left the shop, his mind was set on a course of action. He knew what he had to do, and he was so taken up with the task that he had completely forgotten about Mopsy. His Model A chugged up Broadway to Fifty-fifth Street. Here was a busy intersection which the priest usually tried to avoid. Fifty-fifth Street, a main intersection going north, entered Broadway at a sharp angle. Located in the triangle formed by the conjunction of the two streets was a building that had held a bank which had closed its doors in the economic turmoil of the beginning of the Depression. Behind the bank was the library, its front entrance on Fifty-fifth Street and its back on Broadway. For the priest, making the very sharp, left-hand turn at the library corner was an accomplishment which required both prayer and skill. His method was to put all of his energies into the prayer part. Taking a firm grip on the steering wheel, he rocked his Model A around the traffic signal pedestal in the middle of the intersection, sped in front of a clanging streetcar, and came to a screeching stop in front of the police station opposite the library's main entrance. He was so pleased with himself for having made the turn successfully that he failed to see the sign saying: "Parking for Police Cars Only."

As he stepped out of his car, a uniformed policeman said, "It's against the law not to take your keys, Monsignor."

"Thank you, Mr. Hardy. Is it all right to leave the beast here?"

"Will you be in the station?"

When the priest nodded, the policeman said, "Okay."

Inside the police station, Monsignor Jindra strode up to the sergeant's desk.

"Is Captain Listy still here?" he asked.

"I'm sorry, Monsignor, but you've just missed him."

"Oh," said the priest sadly.

"The lieutenant is here," the sergeant suggested.

"Do I know him?"

"Lieutenant Donnelly, Monsignor?"

"Good!" said the priest. "That's a fine Christian name he has."

Sergeant Novotny pressed a button and said into the intercom, "Monsignor Jindra is here and would like to see you."

"Ask the Reverend Monsignor if he would please come in," came the reply.

The priest winked at the sergeant and whispered, "I can see that his mother brought him up in the faith."

Lieutenant Donnelly was standing in the open door of his office when the priest reached it. With his hand extended, he said, "I'm very pleased to meet you, Monsignor."

The priest returned the greeting and accepted a chair at the policeman's desk as offered. Lieutenant Donnelly sat in his own chair and retrieved a cigar stub from his ashtray and puffed it back into life. The odor of it reminded the priest that he had not had his customary after-dinner cigar. In fact, he had deliberately left his cigars at home so that he could truthfully send Sonny to the store for some. Perhaps the police lieutenant read something in the priest's expression or perhaps the gesture was a customary act of cordiality, but he flipped open a cigar box on his desk and indicated to the priest to help himself if he cared to.

"Are you here to report a crime wave, Monsignor?"

After the first few strong puffs, the priest relaxed in his chair and plunged into the purpose of his visit.

"Has anyone reported the theft or loss of fifteen hundred dollars? Fifteen hundred dollars in tens and fives to be specific?"

Lieutenant Donnelly shuffled through a stack of papers on his desk, shaking his head all the while.

"When? Today?" he asked.

"Perhaps a week ago, more or less."

The lieutenant went through the papers again, more carefully this time.

"Nothing on the blotter. Would the monsignor care to tell me more?"

"Off the record?"

"Absolutely."

"One of my parishioners found that sum of money. In a shoe box it was. One hundred tens and one hundred fives."

"I understand, Monsignor. Frequently, when people find a large sum of money or something very valuable, they turn it over to the pastor of their church." He laughed heartily. "I sometimes think that a policeman's job is to scoop up those that get away from the influence of their church."

Monsignor Jindra was shaking his head because the lieutenant had gone off on the wrong track. The lieutenant interpreted the movements as the priest's way of agreeing, sadly, with him.

"If the monsignor will just give me the package, I'll do the rest."

"Lieutenant, please. You're getting ahead of me. Off the record, remember?"

The policeman nodded.

"You said that no one had reported a theft or a loss?"

"That's correct."

"Does that mean that the finder can in all good conscience keep the money?"

"Yes and no, Monsignor. He should turn it over to the police and let us try to find its rightful owner. After a reasonable time, if no claimant appears, the money is his."

"What if—again the big *if*—what if in all good faith, he should think that the money was rightfully his through the simple act of his finding it? A gift from the leprechauns so to speak. So in all innocence, he spends it?"

Once again the musical laughter of the lieutenant's humor filled the room.

"Leprechauns, to be sure. It's been two dozen years that I've sat upon my mother's knee and heard her weave her magnificent tales of the wee people. 'Tis a lad I wish I were again!"

The priest, knowing that he was in friendly country, stretched out his legs, crossed them at the ankles, and watched a blue smoke ring drift toward the ceiling.

"That's my point, Lieutenant," he sighed. "It was a small boy who found the money, a lad who in the early morning has gathered the wee stools the Little People sat on the night before and who has pulled from the lake the fish that the Little People hooked onto his line. He's a boy good and honest but with a wee bit of the pixy in him."

"In my home there are four just like him," the lieutenant offered understandingly.

"You have four sons? How wonderful."

"No, Monsignor. I have two of each, but my little girls I love like they were sons."

A long pause of silence dimmed the room. Each man pursued his own thoughts for a while. Finally, the priest continued, "The boy told me about his find, not as a secret to be kept, but with the enthusiasm of one who has found the pot of gold at the end of the rainbow. His innocent trust puts me in a very awkward position."

"I can sympathize with your position, but we are both men of the law, ecclesiastical or civil. Both of our actions are directed by laws. In this case, the ecclesiastical and the civil laws are exactly the same."

"Meaning?"

"If the boy doesn't turn the money over to me and if a theft or a loss is reported, I will have to look in your parish for a thief."

"Yes, of course," the monsignor agreed. "But if no theft or loss is reported . . ."

"No crime has been committed as far as the police are concerned until it is a matter of record, or until it has been brought to our attention in some way."

"You're saying that as long as no such report is made, the boy is safe?"

"No, not exactly."

"Exactly what, then?"

"If it should come to my attention that a small boy is spending an awful lot of money, I might investigate the matter to find out where the money came from. My duty compels me to investigate for the possible commission of crimes as well as those that are a part of our records."

"That brings up another point: what about the money he has spent?"

"The monsignor knows the answer. You cannot forgive the sin until restitution has been made. The courts will also insist upon some kind of restitution."

"You are right, Lieutenant. I knew all of the answers before I came here. I'm sorry if I've taken up your time."

"Not at all. You're always welcome. If you need me in this matter, please call."

"No. It's just that this boy for the first time in his life has a dream about to come true. I've got to go and wake him up."

"Are you sure I can't help? Off the record?"

"No, no," the priest lamented, getting to his feet and adjusting his hat. "I've got to do it. It'll be like tripping up my grandmother with two dozen eggs on a slippery sidewalk."

As the priest left the station, he waved good-by to Sergeant Novotny. Executing a fancy U turn, he maneuvered the Model A back onto Broadway and headed back in the direction of the fixit shop. He had to talk this whole thing out with Frank and get the situation resolved before Sonny got a chance to spend some of the money. He knew several people who would be delighted to see Sonny in trouble with the police. He decided that first he would give Frank a chance to save the boy. If that failed, then he would.

Suddenly he saw the subject of his thoughts. There was Sonny coming down the street with Mopsy. Angling to the curb, he beeped his horn. He started to ask Sonny where he was going, but checked himself on seeing the library books. That was good; he could use a few moments alone with the uncle.

"Is Unk back yet?" the priest asked.

Sonny stood on the running board and said, "He's working in the shop on the meat grinder."

A group of small children clustered around the car.

"Give us a ride, Monsignor!" they begged.

He opened the back door and about seven of them

climbed in. Mopsy pushed past them, jumped over the back of the front seat, and took up her co-pilot's position. The boy laughed and waved to all of them.

"Only once around the block," the priest said to the children. "And then home for all of you."

As he drove the allotted distance, the children waved and shouted at friends and passers-by. The priest, oblivious to it all, let his mind dwell on Sonny and the uncle. What he'd have to do was obvious. But there were many other things he could and should do. There were the spectacles, for instance. He could get church funds for them or use his own money. Certainly he would get Frank to an eye doctor. The coat? He'd get one for Frank. He'd ask—no, he'd tell—the St. Vincent de Paul Society to get it. The car? That too would be easy. He was sitting in one and he didn't particularly like the beast. For the rest of the summer, he too would take Wednesdays off. Six o'clock mass on Wednesday and no weddings! He'd ask—no, he'd demand—that Frank take him fishing or mushroom hunting on Wednesdays. He'd tell Frank how much he'd like to go but how he hates to drive. He'd make it sound like Frank was doing him a favor. On some Sunday afternoons they could take a ride also. Maybe the excuse he would use would be that the dog needed the outing. He realized that all this would mean frequent association with Sonny and the breaking of the pledge to himself. But he had to admit that he liked the boy and liked being with him. Also it could mean that as he and Frank spent more and more time together, Sonny would spend less and less with his uncle. He recognized many possibilities to his plan.

"Be honest," he told himself. "You have selfish reasons. You know you'd love to spend a day with Frank and the boy. Fool you are for not having thought of this scheme earlier."

After delivering the giggling children, he made straight for the fixit shop. He found Frank hard at work, filing down the piece of steel to the correct size. He watched the man for a long while. He had heard that da Vinci could draw a perfect freehand circle. Henry Ford and Fred Duesenberg could file a round bar perfectly square. Or they could look at a square piece of metal and know instantly without the use of tools whether it was true on all four sides. Like da Vinci, they held in their minds a true image of the perfect circle or the perfect square, and all they needed to do was to match those images. Novak was in the same class with Ford and Duesenberg. Of course the attainment of such perfection took patience and discipline. Neither da Vinci, nor Ford, nor Duesenberg, nor Novak could accept anything less than the perfect image they carried.

But Frank was talking. He was saying, "The key broke off in the shaft. See how carelessly things are done these days?"

The priest wondered how long Frank had been filing the piece of steel. He would take two or three strokes off one side, rotate the metal, and take two or three strokes off the new side. Finally Frank took the relatively tiny bit of metal out of the vise and held it up to the light. The man's eyes narrowed into slits as he examined all sides of it.

The action gave the priest the opportunity he was looking for although he knew that Frank was using more than eyes to examine his work.

"Either the light in here is bad or you need glasses," he said quietly and good-naturedly.

"I'm not so good as I used to be, but who is?"

The priest sat on the stool and watched the craftsman work. Back into the vise went the metal. Scrape, scrape, scrape, pause, turn the metal, and scrape, scrape, scrape again. Now he checked it. Then he tried it in the slot in the shaft.

"Frank, can you put that aside and talk for a while?"

The uncle was fitting the key into the shaft saying, "Ah, ah, yes, yes. A little more here. Just a tiny bit more off this side."

"Frank!"

"Yes?"

"Can you put that aside and talk for a while?"

"Talk about what?"

"Sonny."

"Go ahead. I can listen while I work."

"He told me about the money, Frank."

"Ah, that's good," the uncle replied but the priest wasn't sure whether he was commenting about the boy or the metal.

"Frank, you can't let the boy keep the money."

"Why? Just a bit more on this side. . . ."

"You can't let him keep it because that will make him into a thief."

"Yes, I know."

"So what are you going to do about it?"

"It? About what?"

"About the money and Sonny. Don't be so exasperating."

"Oh, that," said the uncle. "Nothing."

"Nothing?"

"He'll just have to make up his own mind."

"Frank, Sonny has made up his mind. He's going to spend it."

"Perhaps."

"Perhaps, nothing. He's got it all planned out. You've got to stop him."

"Why don't you?"

"All right, then. I'll do it if I must. But I thought that you as his substitute father would want to do it."

"I'm not worried. You are."

"I don't want my only godson to go to jail," the priest said smilingly but sadly.

The craftsman bent back to his work. He began to file off the end that would project from the shaft. That end would be slightly rounded.

"Frank," said the priest, "this is no small matter."

"No, it isn't. Pasek needs this grinder for tomorrow."

The priest wagged his head sadly. "There must be a hundred or more parishes in the city, why did the likes of you have to move into mine?"

"Now, now, Raymond," the man said soothingly. But his use of the priest's first name was like a shock. No one had called him by his first name for more than a quarter of a century. And yet to hear himself addressed by a name that referred to his childhood gave him a warm feeling. What could he do to a man like that?

"Frank, what are your plans?"

"To finish this blasted thing tonight!"

"You're evading, Frank. You know that I'm talking about Sonny. What are you going to do? Are you going to take that money to the police station?"

"No."

"Why not?"

"Sonny found it. It's up to him."

"Sonny thinks it belongs to him. He thinks that the Little People put it there for him to have."

Frank shrugged and, seeming to be satisfied with his filing, he tore off a strip of emery cloth and began to polish the small piece of metal. Laying the emery cloth flat on the bench, he moved the steel back and forth over it, rotating it periodically. Next he stroked each side on a hone.

"There's a lot more at stake than just a game between you and Sonny. The boy's whole future and yours are involved here."

"You're beginning to sound mysterious."

"Some people want to take Sonny away from you. They think that you're not altogether a good influence on the boy. If Sonny gets into trouble with the police, they may just take him."

"Over my rotting carcass they will," Frank laughed.

"Apparently I'm not getting through to you," complained the priest.

"Maybe it's because I don't know what you're talking about."

"Frank," the priest decided that he was going to knock his idea home. "Some of the people in the parish are getting together to petition the courts to look into your care of the boy. Do you know what that means?"

"It means that someone is looking for a broken jaw."

"Be serious, please."

"Who or why would anyone want to take the boy away from me?"

"They say that you're too lax with the boy for one thing. You act more like a bigger brother than like a father. If Sonny gets into trouble with the police, that's all the proof they'll need. They'll regard that as proof that you're unfit. Worst of all, I may be forced to take their side."

"You'll put your only godson into an orphanage? Every Sunday afternoon you'll visit him with a bunch of bananas?"

"You forget that you have no legal claim to the boy. I'm trying to avoid an investigation before it starts. Everything was between you and me, Frank. There's nothing legal."

"All right then. Let's keep it that way. Just between you and me."

"I don't seem to be getting through to you," the priest repeated mournfully.

The key, being done to Frank's final satisfaction, was laid aside. The craftsman then went to the forge and lit it. As he cranked the fan, the fire became white hot. Picking up the shaft, he stuck the key end into the hot coals.

"I'll get the shaft hot enough to expand the keyway. Then I'll just drop the key into it. When it cools, it will be a snug fit."

The priest watched with mild interest but had no reply. He had momentarily conceded. He thought he'd wait until Frank got the job off his mind. Then possibly the two of them could sit down together and reason out their problem. The thing to do now was to wait until Frank finished what he was doing.

Frank rumbled on about the job, "The trouble was that the key was loose, and it flip-flopped back and forth until the metal weakened. Like you were bending back and forth the lid on a sardine can. The metal fatigues and breaks. If it's a snug fit, the key can't flip-flop."

Seeing a new kind of approach, the priest said, "Isn't the same thing true with boys? Don't you have to apply a little heat now and then? A little pressure so that they don't flip-flop and break?"

"If the metal is good, if it's hardened all the way through and not just case hardened, it'll take all the wear and tear you can give it."

The shaft, where the slot was, turned a bright red. With pliers, the uncle fitted the tiny key into its place. It slid home smoothly. Quenching the reddened end in a bucket of water, he nodded at his work with satisfaction. With his fingers, he tested the fit. The key was locked in place by the contraction of the steel shaft. Taking up the gear, he slid it along the shaft. It moved smoothly until the keyway in the gear met the key. Then it grabbed. The movement displeased the craftsman. Removing the gear, he squinted into the bore. Something he saw annoyed him, and he scowled. With a tiny scraper, he worried at one spot. He tried the gear again. But still the gear failed to slide over the key with the ease with which Frank thought it should. Off came the gear again and received more scraping. After the fourth series, Frank wiped the gear clean, wiped the shaft, and tried again. The gear slid smoothly in place.

"Ah," said Frank.

"I would have banged it with a hammer the first time and have finished the job long ago," the priest commented.

"You never want to hit good steel with a hammer. You've got to coax it along."

"Is it finished now?" asked the priest hopefully.

"It certainly is," the man replied, sliding the gear up and down the shaft. "Now I'll go to Pasek's, put the machine together, and we'll try it. I'll bet that we'll have a meatloaf for dinner tomorrow night."

"That is if you're not in jail tomorrow night along with Sonny."

"Don't be ridiculous!"

"Don't you be a fool!"

"If you're going home, Father, why don't you give me a lift to Pasek's."

"No, I'm not going home until we settle this."

"Okay," said Frank, removing his shop apron and hanging it over the vise. "You stay here and settle things. I'm off to Pasek's."

"Don't go yet!"

"How come?"

"We're going to wait here for Sonny. This matter has got to be settled tonight."

"I'm sorry, but Pasek's waiting."

"Let him wait."

"This thing is important to him. He needs to grind the meat for tomorrow."

"Sonny is more important."

"Sure, but that will keep."

"Tonight," said the priest firmly.

"I don't see why it has to be tonight. Tomorrow will be just as good. The boy's not going to hop a freight."

"Either you or I will take that shoe box to the police station tonight. This game of yours has gone far enough. There's just too much at stake. Sonny's whole future is in our hands."

"Can't you give the boy some time? Can't you let him go to sleep one night a rich man?"

"You're not trying to stall me, are you?" The remark was made humorously to offset Frank's seriousness.

"As a matter of fact I am," the man replied with the same degree of humor. "I've been trying to stall you all evening. But you've been as hardheaded as that dog of yours worrying at a bone."

The priest had forgotten about the dog, but there she was lying by the curtain at the entrance to the kitchen. She was flopped over on her side with her nose in the air, sound asleep.

"All right," agreed the priest. "Tomorrow noon. That will be the deadline."

"Good!" said the uncle.

10

The two men were so interested in their discussion that they failed to notice the arrival of the squad car. It was a big black Peerless sedan with a spotlight mounted on each side of the windshield and a nickel-plated siren on the left front fender. About thirty others just like it were a part of Cleveland's Flying Squad, the police department's high-speed, mobile defense against gangsters and organized crime.

The squad car pulled up smoothly behind the priest's Model A and stopped. A uniformed policeman was at the wheel, and he stayed in the car with its engine running as Lieutenant Donnelly stepped out. The lieutenant spoke briefly to the policeman and helped Sonny get out. The policeman shifted the car into neutral, set the hand brake, and arranged himself comfortably to wait for his superior to return. Sonny then led the way to the shop with the lieutenant close at his heels. The policeman gazed around the neighborhood as if seeing it for the first time. It was still daylight although the sun had already set. He could see people in groups sitting on their front porches, enjoying the cool evening. Neighbors were visiting neighbors, and the policeman sensed, rather than saw, all their eyes turned toward the squad car. He could imagine some of the questions being asked of each other. He would have loved to light up his pipe and to have enjoyed a few puffs, but he was too conscious of being watched.

Sonny opened the door and stepped aside to let the

lieutenant precede him through the door. The priest
flashed an astonished look of recognition at the lieutenant.
There was also accusation in his glance—as Peter must have
looked at Judas. The lieutenant smiled. Mopsy, being
awakened by the opening of the door and recognizing
her playmate, bounded across the floor to greet Sonny as if
they were two old friends.

"Uncle Frank, Monsignor, this is Lieutenant Donnelly,"
Sonny said with sadness.

"Hi," said the policeman.

The two men nodded and looked on quietly.

"I'm going to show the lieutenant the box," the boy
announced glumly. "I'm sorry, Unk, but I think we ought
to do this the right way."

"Yes, of course," said the uncle.

"Maybe there won't be a Ford car, but we've got to do
it right."

The uncle nodded sympathetically.

"When we get a car," the boy went on, "we'll want to
be proud of it. The Novak car has to be an honest car.
It can't be a Holomecz car. Right, Unk?"

"Right!" replied the uncle.

"Like that shaft you've been working on. The right way
only seems harder."

Again the uncle merely nodded, and the boy led the
lieutenant through the shop and into the kitchen. Perhaps
the priest had taken a step to follow them and perhaps
the uncle's hand on his shoulder had caused the priest to
change his mind.

Monsignor Jindra sneaked a quick glance at Frank's
face. The man's jaw was set and his eyes were slightly
moist. The priest wanted to ask the man a lot of questions.
For one thing he would have liked to know what that
"Holomecz" business was all about. The boy was getting

to be like his uncle and was talking in riddles. He wondered what had gone on between the boy and the man since his leaving the boy alone in the shop to go to the police station. What had the uncle done or said that had changed the boy's mind? And did the uncle know what the boy was going to do? Was that why Frank had been stalling? The priest had noticed that the boy had not come in carrying library books. He apparently had dropped them off and had gone across the street to the police station. Had the boy intended to go to the police station all along and was he using the library trip to cover his intentions? He wanted to ask all these questions of Frank, but the conversation in the kitchen stopped him.

"I'm afraid that it's counterfeit," the lieutenant was saying.

"It's no good?" Sonny blurted with a catch in his voice.

"I'm afraid not," the policeman replied. "Look at the serial numbers. The numbers are the same on all the tens. And the fives too."

"They're no good," the boy repeated dazedly.

"See how the ink smears? They didn't even use good ink."

"Just a lot of junk. Nothing but junk!"

"Some member of a gang of counterfeiters must have got scared and ditched it."

"Junk! Lousy junk," Sonny was saying over and over again.

"You're lucky you didn't try to spend any of it," said the policeman by way of trying to console the boy.

"Think of that! A wad of paper not even good enough to write on. Lousy junk!"

"If you had tried to spend any of it, the Secret Service would have been on you like flies on honey."

"Scratch pads I could have used," said the boy. "Not even the box is any good."

"I'll have to take all of it with me," said the lieutenant, "and turn the whole works over to the Secret Service."

"Sure."

"Will you be around tomorrow?"

"Naturally."

"The Secret Service will want you to show them exactly where you found the box."

"Sure, Lieutenant. But ask them if they can't make it in the morning. I've got a ball game to play in the afternoon."

"Oh," said the lieutenant. "Where'll you be playing?"

"We're playing Lourdes at Lourdes at two o'clock."

"I'll ask them to make it in the morning."

"That'll be great."

"If they can't make it in the morning," the lieutenant laughed, "they'll just have to wait until you finish the game."

Sonny laughed with the officer. Then the two of them emerged from behind the curtains. The lieutenant with the box under his arm, walked through the shop and saluted the two men.

"You and I will have to get together someday, Monsignor."

"My parish house is always open," said the priest.

The lieutenant saluted again and stepped out into the evening which had grown dark. The two men could see the headlights flash against the window as the squad car sped away. The bare bulb over Frank's bench cast yellowish shadows about the room. The boy had scooped up the dog and had returned to the kitchen.

"I guess I would have used a hammer," the priest said as a self-accusation. "You just don't pound good steel."

Gently the uncle took the priest by the arm and guided

him into the kitchen. Sonny was on his bed with the dog in his lap. His cheek was against the thick hair around the dog's neck.

"I'm sorry, Unk," the boy said when he saw them enter. "No Ford car. Who would think that the Little People would have left me a boxful of junk. Just lousy junk. But we had a good game."

"You can't come up with mushrooms or elderberries all the time," the uncle replied.

"I have an idea," the priest said brightly. "Why don't you take my car on Wednesdays? Take the car and the dog and go out into the country. That mutt needs some exercise. Maybe sometime you'll let me go with you. I might like to go fishing or mushroom hunting, but I hate to drive."

The boy was gently stroking the dog's fur from her neck to the tip of her tail. Mopsy, to show her appreciation for the attention, turned her head upward and licked him under the chin.

"Anthony," said the uncle gently.

Slowly the boy took his attention from the dog and fastened it on his uncle. He had been called by a name that only the sisters had used. Puzzled, he put the dog aside and sat up straight.

"In Pasek's tonight, Anthony," the uncle began, "I met Mr. Stanek. He used to work with me a long time ago in the mill. He used to be one of my apprentices. Now he's the master mechanic. He says that the mill is beginning to start up again and he needs another mechanic to help him get the machinery going again."

"He picked the right man," said Sonny. "There's no better. He must know it if he learned from you."

"I've taken the job, Anthony. I'll start tomorrow."

"You're the best, Unk."

"Do you know what that means?"

"Yes, sir."

"You'll have to stay here by yourself all day and fix your own lunch."

"I can be your cook. I'll get your breakfast and fix supper. You'll have to eat my dumplings for a change."

"When school starts, you'll have to get yourself off. Can you do it?"

"Sure, Unk. I'm grown up."

"The pay is good," said the uncle. "We'll have to start thinking about getting you outfitted for school."

"The glasses," the boy objected. "The glasses come first. I don't want to have to worry about your thumb getting cut off."

"I'll get the glasses. The very first payday I'll go see Dr. Mikesh."

"And an overcoat for you?"

"I'll get a lousy stinking overcoat if you'll only stop nagging me about it," the uncle laughed.

"Good! I refuse to go to church with you in wintertime unless you have an overcoat. A mechanic like you should have an overcoat."

"Maybe someday," the uncle continued, "we can live in a house."

"I like it here. You can keep up your fixit shop and teach me to be a mechanic. When I'm sixteen, I'll quit school and go to work. I could be your best apprentice."

"There'll be no quitting school," said the uncle firmly. "I'd rather grind you up and feed you to the lions at the zoo than let you quit school. You'll go to school until you graduate. Then maybe you'll even go some more."

"Yes, sir."

The priest, who had been wrapped up in the conversation, suddenly said, "What about my idea about taking the car and exploring the countryside?"

"It's great," said Frank.

"We'll make you into a fisherman," said the boy. "You may even become a scrounger and learn the difference between a mushroom and a toadstool."

"Now I've got to get this thing over to Pasek's," Frank said.

"Take my car," said the priest. "I'd rather walk home. Just leave it out in front of your place and I'll pick it up in the morning after mass."

"Won't you need it?"

"I think not. It'll give me an excuse to stop in and check to see how Sonny's doing as the downstairs maid."

"Okay, then. Good night, Raymond."

"Good night, Frank."

When the door had banged behind the uncle, the priest said to the boy, "If you'll give me my dog back, I'll go home. I'm pretty tired."

"Did you have a busy day, Father?"

"I don't really think so. I certainly didn't accomplish much. But the day was interesting."

"Don't you think Unk took everything nicely? He's a real champ."

"Yes, he's a real champ."

"He knew all along that I'd have to take the money to the police station, and yet he never told me to do it."

"He didn't?" asked the priest because this was one of the questions puzzling him.

"Well, maybe he did in a way."

"In what way?"

"I guess you'll have to ask him to tell the story of stupid Holomecz," said the boy and laughed heartily.

"Come on, Mopsy," the priest said. "Folks in this house have gone crazy."

"All fishermen go crazy like that, Father. Do you still want to go with us?"

"I'll go only because your uncle's stories may do me some good. I may be able to get some sermons out of them."

Outside, with Mopsy trotting after him, he strolled through the cool evening toward home. He felt good. The boy had proved to be more than he might have hoped for him. The forty-two dollars were still in his pocket which made him feel sad in a way. "I guess they really don't need me," he told himself. "Well, that's good. They're a tough pair, bless them."

As he turned into Broadway, he almost knocked Baba Chlepna over. He wondered where she had been. Had she been sitting on someone's front porch, keeping a watch on Frank's place?

"Did you see that, Monsignor?" Her voice was filled with exaggerated horror. "A squad car brought Sonny home. I told you so. I just knew that that boy would get himself into serious trouble."

"You'd better get back here early tomorrow morning or you'll miss the Secret Service agents who are coming to pick him up."

"Oh, my goodness! Is it all that bad?"

"The Secret Service just doesn't come around making social calls," the priest said, enjoying himself tremendously.

"What is it, Monsignor? You can tell me. You know how much I'm interested in that boy. What has he done?"

"Quite a bit, I guess."

"Oh," and she clicked her tongue sorrowfully. "What terrible thing could it have been?"

"Why, Mrs. Hronek, what makes you so sure that it was terrible?"

"The police brought him home in a squad car."

"Sonny's done nothing wrong," the priest said gently. "As a matter of fact, he's helping the police solve a very important crime. And tomorrow he will assist the Secret Service in its investigation."

"Oh, how wonderful!" she gushed. "Is it something I know about?"

"I doubt it," said the priest deliberately whetting her curiosity for the purpose of letting it hang there. "Maybe someday it will come out in the papers. But you know what the Secret Service means."

"What, Monsignor, does it mean?"

"It means that its business is secret."

As he turned to leave her, he said, "I think that you had better stop in at the parish house tomorrow after eight o'clock mass. There's something I'd like to say about your activities in relation to the Novaks."

"Yes, Monsignor."

"Good night, and may God go with you."

RICHARD E. DRDEK grew up in the Cleveland he describes in THE GAME and went to college there at Cleveland State University. He joined the Air Corps after Pearl Harbor as a navigator and his plane crashed in the jungles of northern Brazil. Four days later, his crew, escaping serious injury, was rescued by a Navy blimp. After this exciting military career, he returned to civilian life and received a Master of Science degree in education. He has taught in the classroom and has written beginning reading books. At present he is Assistant Professor of Elementary Education at the New York State University College at Brockport. THE GAME is his first book for children in the middle grades.